SMOKE AND MIRRORS:
POLICE DREAMS

Smoke and Mirrors: Police Dreams

A Literary Painting

JORDAN P. CASTRO

Library of Congress Control Number:		2016911284
ISBN:	Hardcover	978-1-5245-2444-9
	Softcover	978-1-5245-2443-2
	eBook	978-1-5245-2442-5

Print information available on the last page.

Rev. date: 09/23/2016

To order additional copies of this book, contact:
Xlibris
1-888-795-4274
www.Xlibris.com
Orders@Xlibris.com
744852

DEDICATION

To my mother, who gave me the gift of a heartbeat and defined love for me since my first breath. If I could be like anybody in this world I would be like you.

To my father, who has always guided me and kept me motivated. You could have stopped at little league but instead you coached me through life.

To the love of my life, Angelique: my soul found yours amidst a universe of souls and we will dance together everlastingly. Your love sustains me, elevates me, and is the reason why I push so hard.

To our gorgeous daughter, Evangeline: your birth was the happiest moment of my life. I can't imagine existing without you in this world and I will give you the world in return for your love—and that precious smile.

Thank you to my generous sister, Shanna, and inspirational brother, David, as well as my extended family in the NYPD. I started with two siblings and now I have thousands. From the 4-8 to the 2-5 to PSA 7 and every stop in between, it has been an honor to follow in the footsteps of coach Johnny from the Michael J. Buczek Little League and serve this amazing city. For the hometown heroes of Bronx Housing IRT ("ask about them"), and those in Dallas, Baton Rouge and all over the United States, I dedicate this book to your service and your sacrifice. Thank you. You are the thin blue line.

CHAPTER I

This gets ugly before it gets beautiful. At times, the two will be swirled together and dispensed out like some sort of delicious, revolting oil-acrylic mix. There is a Rose at the center of this tale; his petals are pretty but he has thorns too—a palette's worth of them. I don't say this as a preamble to foreshadow some type of obvious dualism but rather to remind you that human beings are breathing contradictions, and police officers—quite obviously—are human beings. A police officer can be wild or he can be cultivated. Six months of having the patrol guide and the New York State Penal Law shoved down your throat while running in circles at the police academy's stifling gym neither creates nor kills a cowboy. It is what he does during his tours on the streets that will define him as a trigger-happy racist or a compassionate hero. And although you may assert that there is a rigid dichotomy separating the two, I am here to correct you and disprove the mutual exclusivity of these things.

The NYPD is a diverse amalgam and its officers come in a cornucopia of colors, hues, shades, and tints—just like a rose. For the purpose of this investigation, visualize a deep crimson Rose, similar in color to a dead man's blood, after a bullet ripped his lid open and left him bleeding out on a frigid Bronx street. While you're at it, imagine a whimsical wind dancing fickly around him—like electrons prancing around a nucleus—freezing his life force over gradually and unevenly on the speckled pavement where his perforated remains lie. And then the languishing locals, heedlessly attempting to *limbo* under black and yellow crime scene tape, asking jaded, sleep-deprived officers working unwanted overtime, "Can I pass, officer? Why can't I pass?" This as the altar bells of Ash Wednesday Mass ring faithfully, ahead of the Consecration, awakening churchgoers' wandering minds and signaling that a miracle was about to take place.

Do not get too distracted by the details of the aforementioned scenario—particularly the ringing bell. It is a *smoke* screen. We are still talking about a blood red Rose: warm, loving, passionate; one who epitomizes the heart's manifold mysteries. Well, this individual was hired by the world-renowned NYPD in the summer of 2006 and this is how his mercurial career unfurled.

It was the first day of Lent 2007. It had been three years since the advent of a certain social media behemoth and just three months after a Queens man was regrettably fired upon fifty times outside of a titillating tit joint on Ninety-fourth Avenue in Jamaica, Queens. If you recall, that was the year that everyone knew exactly how they would respond in high-stress, life and death situations, all while taking cover from exploding bullets behind their coffee tables and keyboards. It was the Genesis of the Internet "Police Era" and the commencement of some very burdensome times for law enforcement officers. A period that would encompass a horrific double assassination in New York City and the deadly ambush in Dallas, precipitated by questionable police-involved shooting fatalities in Baton Rouge and Minnesota.

On the evening of February 21^{st,} an evening of purported fasting as it was Ash Wednesday, the probationers were patrolling the filthy streets. Sex wasn't supposed to be in the air, but it was—and it had a stench to it. The entire stairwell smelled like a queer concoction of cannabis and crotch, and it wafted—waltzed even—through the weighty air. This was before bullets were in the air and then all the air came completely out of the evening; the night itself caving in badly and fatally coughing up blood on the high gloss shoes of the next day's dawn. Era-wise, this was *before* anyone "couldn't breathe," when we weren't foolishly arguing about whose life mattered. Criminals were still bad, cops were still good, and "body-cam" was a fetal neologism that had not yet entered the law enforcement lexicon. No, back then the only thing on a cop's shirt was his badge, his commendation bars, longevity marks, the distinct NYPD patch, and perhaps some cream cheese or mayonnaise from eating on the run because he was always running to save somebody's life. It was a time when they had not yet poisoned the atmosphere or falsified the narrative and a young, ambitious, quixotic officer still held tightly to his police dreams. On this particular night Officer Fernandez held tightly to Officer Smith's twenty-three-inch waist as if that was his police dream.

Smith was porcelain-skinned, stunning to sight, and had taken off her bullet resistant vest on the soiled roof landing of the building in which she was supposed to be conducting a vertical patrol. She was bobbing enough to almost entirely erase the black, powdery ash cross—made from blessed palm branches—that a Catholic priest had rubbed on her forehead earlier that day. Fernandez was doing what training officers sometimes did with the attractive rookies that they were entrusted to train, which is to penetrate them. He was selected by the lieutenant to penetrate their minds with his wealth of police wisdom, but he periodically found his way into their erogenous zones for an alternate type of puncturing. He certainly looked sleazy. Tanning bed bronze in color, his hair was lush, ink-black and oily, preserved immaculately in a gelled-to-the-side coiffure. He grabbed a fistful of Smith's corkscrewed curls while cupping her milky white left tit and massaging her nipple in between his middle finger and ring finger. The coldness of his yellow metal wedding ring chilled her nipple and hardened it, making its bullet-like shape more pronounced. She did not notice the grime underneath his fingernails, or repel from the residual onion and garlic taste on his slippery tongue as it twisted in her mouth and she twisted her head back and kissed him deeply. She merely reciprocated his thrusts as they banged away into the tragic night before the Central dispatcher interrupted their rooftop rendezvous with a staticky message.

"Five-one posts nine and ten, are you still out on that vertical patrol?" Central asked.

Central was simply checking the "overdues": cops who transmitted an assignment but had not yet given back the final disposition and thirty minutes had elapsed. Neither Naomi Smith nor Noel Fernandez were in any position to respond to her considering their radios were on their gun belts, right next to their tactical pants and their morals, on the ground. Lust had the law in a state of temporary unavailability.

A few blocks away, urine streams splashed off uneven roof tar as the most curious pair of cops I've ever had to investigate performed foot patrol against the swirly, Van Gogh-imagined nocturne. Subject one: with his broad back to the world, slicked-back hair protruded from the rim of a police officer's eight-point hat. That hair was neatly tapered, blended to perfection by a pot-smoking Dominican barber's steady hand, resulting in a flawless fade. The hair adorned the head of Icarian police officer Brandon Rose. Rose was handsome for a cop and possessed an ochre glint in his predominantly brown eyes that was bordering on a flame. He was twenty-six by the time his case folder slid demandingly across my desk, but if not for the shadow on his face from skipping a shave every other day he could have passed for a teenager. Rose was short in stature, but filled out his uniform muscularly. Although he was a professional, he was still mischievous enough to take a leak on a rooftop in full NYPD uniform.

And then there was his partner, subject two: a witty and unwitting foil to Rose, going by the nickname "Cheddar." Two months in, he was already an established "hair bag." Cheddar was tall, lanky, and awkward, possessing no discernible haircut. His uniform looked deliberately missized, and he found it impossible to keep his shirt tucked in. The young man was the personification of a pig's ear and fundamentally opposed to obsequiousness. Cheddar didn't give a crap about NYPD rules or appearance regulations; he barely gave a crap about God.

"So you're telling me with all the vile, despicable shit that you see here you actually still believe in God?" he needled, his jadedness carried proudly in his voice and its soupy, accented way of stringing words together without a pause.

A meditative Rose avoided looking at Cheddar and instead stared at the medallion-like moon, which hung over the purpling sky—with its pastel apricot streaks—like a sentinel keeping watch. Rose punctually reviewed his religious values and his ethics and replied, "If it's all right with you I'd rather not talk about God while my dick is in my hands."

"My dick is always in my hands," Cheddar embellished. "That's why I'm silent on the man above."

"*I'm* not silent on him. But now isn't the time," Rose deferred.

Rose shifted his feet and his polished black boots crunched the glass of the strewn syringe needles that lay beneath him, remnants of a junkie's reality-departing rituals at some earlier point of the doomed day. Pigeons *cooed* and shat, peppering the building ledge with green and white slime in which, when the night was over and done, everybody would be covered. Cheddar challenged his associate.

"Now's probably the best time to talk about God. Considering how he took a holy piss on us and made us lowly cops."

"Look, we're lowly cops *now*, but don't think for a second that there isn't still prestige in wearing this uniform," Rose rebutted superiorly. "Plus, if you don't like where you're at, you can always move up. I know I am. I'm getting my detective's shield. Gold shield or bust for me."

Rose's climber's zeal was off-putting if only because his ambition was so naked for someone at such an immature stage of his career.

Cheddar picked his nose at Rose's prophesy and dismissively wondered to himself where the adjoining post of Fernandez and Smith had been hiding all night.

That hiding place was the romping roof landing where their bodies were acquainting themselves and now reaching the zenith of their passion's climb. Their shadows moved erotically against a graffiti-covered wall that read "fuck the police" and "Jeu $aves." I tried translating the double entendre, the latter one that is, as the former was too literal to miss. Did our Lord and Savior put away his pennies or was money the new God and therefore what was worshipped here? You would not have been able to unscramble it anyway over the crisp sound of flesh smacking flesh as Fernandez and Smith coalesced in orgasmic synchrony. Their intermittent grunts and gasps dwindled into barely audible throaty offerings of sound to convey satisfaction and depletion. A post-coital embrace took place amidst piss-soaked newspaper sales circulars and decomposing blunt wrappers.

Smith, feeling very much used and looking for immediate redemption asked—with the clarity that after-climax often provides, "Now can you train me on how to stop, question, and frisk a suspect?" Fernandez simply nodded, looking over the pieces of his uniform scattered on the ground the way rookie officers were scattered throughout the neighborhood, none receiving anywhere near the amount of individual attention that he paid to Smith and her burgeoning loins.

There was a stash house within the very same building—a lair for three ruthless drug dealers who had become notorious in the area for administering violence. On this day, a Thanksgiving feast-sized bundle rested on the table including seven thousand bags of heroin, twenty thousand bags of marijuana, and a skyline of rubber-banded money stacks, beautifully and asymmetrically arranged. There were four guns on the table as well, with duct tape securing the magazine to the handle in order to make them operable. Incongruously, a newscaster on the local channel reported a precipitous drop in crime, possibly a result of new report-taking techniques that brought a whole new meaning to the term "shit-canning." Let's just say that New York's Strongest might have been picking up a few more opaque bags of neatly shredded paper from the city's belittered sidewalks.

"Crime is down to historic lows in the Big Apple, with rapes, homicides, and robberies seeing the most significant drop-offs," reported some mustachioed stiff on the Bronx News Channel.

On their now-christened rooftop, Rose and Cheddar terminated their conversation on the Lord and their ambitions within the department. Rose removed his eight-point hat and tucked it under his armpit, revealing a dark, ashen cross, slightly smeared.

"Holy shit! You have a shit stain on your forehead. One of them pigeons gave you a facial," Cheddar blasphemed gleefully.

"That's incredibly funny. Heathens never say things like that, right? I hope your stand-up comedy act serves you well in the ninth circle of hell with Satan the Devil drilling you softly with his pitch fork dick," replied Rose, vulgarly embodying a demon thrusting.

"What?" Cheddar volleyed. "This is hell. And I just marked my own little corner of it. I wish I could give the entire Bronx a golden shower. I put in for Midtown South. I'd take a shit on this place if I could. There's nothing good here, and the longer we stay here, the quicker we rot."

Rose was preparing his hopeful rebuttal when the night made a much more emphatic statement than he ever could have.

BANG! BANG! BANG! BANG! BANG! BANG! The cadence of the claps was both binary and booming. Pigeons scattered into the air like packs of feathered fireworks. Rose and Cheddar instinctively reached for their firearms trying to determine in which direction they needed to run.

Fernandez and Smith needed only to run down the stairs as the gunfire was coming from below them. She looked at him the way a fawn caught on railroad tracks would look at a stag as a locomotive approached; the night itself now moving with muscular locomotion and becoming a graffiti-covered runaway train.

The dispatcher spat out information for anybody with a radio hanging off their gun belt: "At this time, within the confines of the *five-one* precinct I'm receiving multiple calls of numerous shots fired from inside of 1805 Harmony Avenue. Awaiting description at this time. Do I have any units in the area?"

Smith buttoned up her blouse while a partially clad Fernandez handled the communication.

"This is five-one post nine, Central. Be advised, we heard about six shots fired from one of the lower floors. Give me an eighty-five forthwith!"

Two last, loud, echoing reports produced more human rubble as all the personnel of the fifty-first precinct converged on 1805 Harmony Avenue like a big, blue tidal wave. No one yet knew that a tectonic shift had taken place—an earthquake that moved them collectively and seismically to the scene of the Ash Wednesday massacre and its momentous fallout.

Two men had asserted themselves violently inside of an apartment that night—the very apartment in which the newscaster previously informed that New Yorkers were safer than ever. Their street monikers were "Diablo" and "Kilo," but I later ascertained their names were Alejandro Salazar and Ernesto Castillo. The description broadcast on that day was "two male blacks wearing dark-colored hoodies, blue jeans, black Timberland-type construction boots, and skulls caps." The first 911 caller was an elderly lady named Josephina Beltran who had the perfect line of rollers in her thinning hair unceremoniously undone by the seventh bullet fired by the assailants. Her powder blue, large-sized curling rollers hit the floor, crimsoned with blood, even before her face slammed into the tiles on the unmopped corridor floor. Grouped strands of hair came uncoiled after the firearms recoiled and then Diablo fired the eighth shot of the sequence into her spine, assuring that her eighty-fifth year on earth would be her final.

A size 10 rubber sole footprint was left in blood for crime scene investigators to hypothesize over. The apartment of the initial crime was converted into a butcher's slaughterhouse. Narcotics and dirty money were drenched in a thick, purplish-red fluid. Three victims inside were obliterated, saturated in blood to the point where their clothing and their skin appeared to fuse into one. A ceiling fan spun and spritzed the apartment in some type of inadvertent spiral-patterned death drizzle, the whirly blades chopping through the grave air, chilling the chilling scene even more.

Fernandez kicked the door in as he and Smith arrived, guns pointed and fingers riding the triggers. Smith surveyed her first crime scene and reactively vomited all over it. Fernandez pulled out his radio to transmit and blood leaked onto his cheek from above. Rose and Cheddar soon converged on the scene and inspected the macabre blood bath for themselves.

As police raced to the scene, an anti-cop mob organically formed outside the housing development. At first, they merely observed the police response but soon they taunted responding officers and eventually hurled trash at them, plucked from a nearby receptacle, which was later set aflame. It was dizzying how counterintuitive this was to me. But when two blue and white police vehicles careened onto the scene, the gang surrounded the vehicles and pushed the officers down as they attempted to exit their *RMP*s. Officer Jade and Officer Fable grabbed their shiny black batons and created some space for themselves. Officer Fable then *suplexed* some delinquent that thought it would be humorous to steal his cap from him, depositing him on the dog shit side of a short chain link fence. This as bottles, rocks, and other debris began to rain down on them like execrable precipitation. The veterans unwantedly put on a batting practice-worthy display that night. Polycarbonate collided with calcium carbonate, adding to the profuse blood spilled on the first day of Lent. Rioters crumbled to the concrete, police stepping over their anatomies in order to enter the building to try and apprehend the ostentatious outlaws. Cops were knocked unconscious, but backup broke bones on the ribcages of resisters. A cinder block crashed from out of the night sky like a cop-seeking meteorite, crunching the roof of a marked police vehicle and decimating the turret lights, spraying red and blue shards onto the mixed media canvass.

Officers painted the swarm with pepper spray, commonly and incorrectly referred to as *mace*. Onlookers yelled "police brutality" but what was brutal was that two murderous assailants were allowed to escape by a community who would rather intervene in police action than aid officers in investigating a crime in progress by offering even a sliver of useful information. A beer bottle cracked on an officer's head as *fuck the police* chants could be heard, sung proudly by onlookers in the streets. Rose transmitted his emergency message with as much composure as possible:

"Five-one post seven, Central: I need four buses over here, I still need additional units! I need the patrol supervisor, ESU, I need the whole goddamn world here, Central!"

Amidst the maelstrom, a petite teenage terror zigzagged through the crowd and the cops, sliding past a guarding officer as if on roller skates and entering the closed off lobby of the hive-like building. She whizzed past police lines with a ballerina's grace and scampered up scummy steps. The glimpse I got of her was brief, but her large brown eyes haunt me to this day. She carried a *Hanna Montana* book bag and a sense of responsibility, her urgency perceivable in the kinesics of her body. She wasn't just a nosy neighbor; she was there to facilitate.

Task Force eventually arrived, donning disorder control helmets, straight batons, and pissed off Bronx attitudes. They quickly turned the turbulent tide, relegating the rioters to remnants and dismantling the resistance. Twenty-three people were arrested in the clash; at least fifty tasted some aspect of police weaponry. But not a single shot was fired by officers. Not a single civilian was killed after the initial massacre. The evening had caved in disastrously. The murderers presumably rode the tide out like the trough, and almost everyone who was there was revealingly covered in ashes or blood or bird shit.

> *"When the sun wakes to sorrow, a tired new day yawns against the backdrop of musty, stagnant curtains that destitution wove. The sun scans for braver clouds to hide behind, fearing its light will expose the embedded grime in this tattered urban tapestry."*

Pounding jackhammers clamorously blasting up pavement, first responders' sirens, honking vehicles, unruly vagrants rising from alcohol comas, the *"aye yooooo!"* of a street hustler's morning bustle—you might have experienced all of these niceties on your way to 235 East 20th Street. That is where Officer Rose first trained in the delicate art of policing. An occupation that is so widely scrutinized today that some officers are actually afraid to protect themselves from combative violators for fear of being investigated, sued or arrested. Force never looks pleasant on video but, then again, when was the last time you saw someone throw an elbow, a kick, or club someone with an expandable baton at the home stage of Lincoln Center for the Performing Arts? This is a dirty, dirty profession, which is to say you will be on the ground a lot, fighting like a dog. Just because someone isn't armed doesn't mean that they can't take your gun away from you and send you home to your family in a mahogany box so the local newspapers can appoint you to hero.

Now the first time in his young career that Rose truly swelled with inspiration, according to the information I've collected, was when Sergeant McMahon gave his hallmarked speech following the second week of tactics training in the police academy gymnasium. McMahon was a tall, muscular, freckled, Irish alpha male with biceps that stretched his NYPD polo and a whistle that he would blow the pea out of to settle the rowdy recruits.

"Bring it in, you filthy animals! Week two is in the books; you're that much closer to receiving your guns and shields. That doesn't mean you turn into Rambo and shoot every single thing that moves. This isn't hunting, this is *policing*. Your most powerful tools are your *mind*, and by that I mean the ability to make quick, sound decisions. Your *voice*, your *hands*, and then—if that doesn't work—you have options on your Batman utility belt to get someone to comply. If you are in imminent fear of serious physical injury or death—this means someone charges at you with a knife, a bat, points a gun at you, you have the power to shoot that person and arrange their meeting with the big guy upstairs. We do not ever shoot to kill; we shoot to stop the threat. But if you shoot someone in their chest, where their vital organs are located, I'm pretty sure their ticket is gonna be stamped one-way. They probably ain't comin' back from that. This is where you should be aiming," McMahon illustrated, making a circular motion over his chest and abdomen. "Unless you want to aim for their leg, miss, hit grandma, and end up with a rusty steak knife in your eye socket. I don't know about you, but I like my green eyes."

The recruits respected McMahon, but Rose admired him even more so. He remembered him fondly from the beer-assisted, sun-kissed softball games on rock-filled fields during NYPD family day. McMahon didn't recognize Rose; he was just another face in a crowd which included youthful faces, a few pimpled faces, apparitions, and apples hanging off an imaginary bough as wet as can be. But there was Rose and his focused, intense, determined eyes and his *name* printed in bold blue letters across his shirt. He should have stood out. It was surprising that McMahon didn't make the connection.

"Don't you ever forget that this job is dangerous. Sometimes, we don't make it home to our families," McMahon delivered almost as a mnemonic, or like an actor hitting his marks. "Don't ever let it slip from your minds the ultimate sacrifice that some of our brothers and sisters made in dying in the line of duty. On my prompt, everybody here give me twenty pushups for our blue angels in the sky who watch over us as we protect and serve."

Rose performed the pushups with perfect form and fervor. His eyes took in all the bronze plaques commemorating slain officers, which hung in a row like a monument park of NYPD hall of famers. His sweat concealed the salty liquid forming in those eyes as he pumped out pushups and traced the badge number of Detective First Grade Reinaldo "Great Ray" Rose with the glassy windows to his bruised soul. McMahon would go on to end every week with this type of *in memoriam* and every week Rose would build his muscles and leave a little piece of his heart on that sweaty gym floor.

Six months evanesced like vapor and by the time Rose, Cheddar, and numerous other rookie officers emerged from the murky, smoky corridor in the dank bowels of the fifty-first precinct on their orientation day, they already had adversaries on the streets who were preparing for them. As Rose made the sign of the cross in front of a religious fraternity poster of St. Michael, patron saint of police officers, Jefferson Greer and Jonathon "Puff" Gibson were tucking black Glock pistols into their waistbands and also requesting divine protection via the sign of the cross. These two men had garish gold and diamond Jesus medallions dangling off their necks as well as red *due-rags* which were very much in style at the time. The Son of God's eyes were replaced with diamond studs which created the obvious pun on "diamond vision." The marriage of Jesus and jewels or Christ and cash seemed out of place, given the drug-peddling profession that currently employed the two and surely wasn't in favor with the Roman Catholic Church. But if you have ever visited a Catholic church, you quickly realized that the Lamb of God and the root of all evil have been going hand in hand since the advent of Catholicism. Rose and his colleagues had to settle for the redeemer and pass on the riches because at a mere $25,100 per year salary they wouldn't be buying diamond encrusted Jesus pieces anytime soon. And so they had to work, long and hard, and the prayer quote next to the St. Michael poster that read "Lord, protect us for we are police officers" was very much necessary at this point.

Greer and Puff could make an officer's salary in one month, and they would readily test God's ability to provide the prayed for protection if a cop tried disrupting their thriving pharmaceutical enterprise. Rose hadn't met them yet—he wouldn't on this day either—but he wouldn't allow anything to stand in the way of arriving home safely to his beloved Cecelia. She was light and life, melody and mate, and upon making it home to her that afternoon—one of the few times he worked during the daytime—he turned off all the lights and illuminated his apartment with one hundred cotton-wicked, white tea light candles, neatly arranging them in the form of a colossal question mark. Rose was meticulous and took painstaking care to line up the diminutive candles evenly and in perfect configuration, so they could light up the living room the way she set fire to his romantic heart.

"Cecelia, can you come over here for a second?" he requested sweetly.

Cecelia Cruz had the largest, most beautiful, dewy brown eyes to ever introduce a soul. She possessed long, flowing, dark hair which cascaded down from the vermillion headband that she habitually wore while devouring books in bed. Rose did not wait for her to use her perfectly toned legs to travel to him as he swooped over and whisked her into the living room to decipher his fiery formation.

"Okay, okay. This question mark means . . . you're questioning your career choice?" she playfully asked. A bashful grin stretched out across her face as she batted her sumptuous eyelashes at her boyfriend in a way that was concurrently flirty and sheepish. Rose, never breaking eye contact, dropped to one knee and presented her with a black leather camera case divided into quadrants by a spindly pink ribbon.

She half-jokingly offered, "You finally got me the upgrade I wanted?" and Rose confessedly punned.

"I've upgraded you all right, from my girlfriend to my fiancée."

Cecelia was unable to pick her feet up following this revelation, her legs becoming pudding-like and quaking beneath her. She wasn't expecting a gift of this magnitude considering Rose had already paid for her plane ticket to study in the Golden Gate City. When Rose opened the box for her, a large diamond ring sparkled, reflecting the fire of his candle creation and reflecting their love in both its size and clarity. And then suddenly heat and passion and love impacted their embrace in the center of their living room, in the middle of a moment that would belong to them forever, even if everything else would decay around them like acidic teeth in a bacteria-filled mouth.

This night, however, displayed nothing but the healthy teeth of their luminous smiles, which tested the endurance of their cheek muscles.

"I'm assuming your answer is yes?" Rose wagered, requesting confirmation to commence the celebration and uncork the freezing *demi-sec* bubbly.

"Yes! Yes! Yes! How can I say no? You'll probably burn the house down if I do," she teased, employing her balmy charm in tandem with her ravishing physicality .

"Oh baby, I'm about to burn this city down. We're engaged! And . . . my first day on the streets is tomorrow!" he rejoiced, his life seemingly falling into place, at least on the veneer.

"My flight is tomorrow," she reminded, throwing down the obligatory wet blanket.

The newly-betrothed couple looked deeply and despondently into each other's eyes—familiar as the mirror. A conversation ensued in which Cecelia questioned Rose's decision to be a cop. He reminded her that being a cop was better than his other option of being a teacher in the public school system, where kids come to class with guns, but the Board of Education doesn't provide its educators with bullet resistant vests.

"Your bullet proof vest is for . . .?"

"High fashion," he cut in. "But for those who want to do us harm we have a knife-proof tie and bite-proof crotch protector."

"Oh I really need that crotch of yours protected," she insisted in her resonantly kittenish manner.

Rose assured her he would protect all the parts of his body, from his fingers to his toes and everything in between. He placed his forefingers underneath her earlobes, gingerly caressing her cheeks with his thumbs, and pulling her entrancing, svelte face toward him. He placed his lips on hers and breathed her in entirely before producing the suction necessary to deliver an actual kiss. He transferred the love from his soul to hers and hugged her, shaking her slightly as if to galvanize her heart into feeling exactly what he felt at that precise moment.

"I promise you, love of my life, that I will not come home in any worse condition, or with any more holes in my body, or any more fractured than when I left the house. And when you are done with school and we are together again, I will marry you in a church, before God."

Rose wasn't endeavoring to sound dramatic, that was just him. He was theatrical and idealistic and intended, like hell, to honor his promise. He loved her with all the strength in his body, its warm blood delivered by a gigantic, over-pulsating, nurturing heart that was so uncommon for a man to possess in this day and age. He was like a male mother; he could love so much it would become a defect. And he would be contending with distance and time for the next two years as she studied in California and he began one of the most perilous and life-draining careers in the United States. For these reasons I believe that Brandon Rose, *subject one*, was a tragedy restlessly waiting to happen. And so I watched him closely, from his infancy to his incandescence, never taking my eyes off this beautiful, meteoric man. It was the greatest assignment of my career in this goddamn bureau before I put in my retirement papers only to live life as an uncompensated lessee in a house of unremitting torment and revisitation.

CHAPTER II

In a Bronx stash house apartment long, flat-ironed, raven black hair framed the striking face of a troubled teenage girl. Expressive, large, carnivorous chocolate brown eyes emerged, enhanced by the charcoaled effects of smoky eye makeup. Her name was Giselle Ignacio, sixteen years old and sopping with sex appeal—the kind that could land a man in a jail cell if he didn't properly card the bait. Her *Hanna Montana* backpack rested at the foot of the couch, and on this evening she halfheartedly perused *The Catcher in the Rye,* creating a sort of delightful cognitive dissonance with everything else drunkenly orbiting around her. The smoke she exhaled from her voluptuous, reddened, desirous lips was the product of a marijuana cigarette that she could roll with the expertise of a Cuban tobacconist since about the age of twelve. Her exhaust dissipated into the air like a ghost struck by a tennis racket as she raised her artfully arched, tweezer-touched eyebrows and enjoyed a sip of dark cognac that was the drink of preference in similar *households* throughout the Bronx. She was comfortable in her taut, oily skin and after placing her beverage down she casually ran her fingers through the coarse hair in between her legs. Giselle massaged her pubic area with the Skittles-colored nails of a French manicure, embellished by a glued-on imitation diamond on the nail of each ring finger. She was precocious, flagrantly and unapologetically *ghetto,* and still she possessed a spunky charisma and sneaky intellect that the men currently in her presence took for granted.

Greer and Puff had just concluded playing football on a video game console when they changed the input list to their cable television. Surprisingly, and because of Giselle's doing, the last channel was a news channel which happened to be covering the New York City police academy graduation ceremony, which had just concluded. Giselle placed down her book, somewhat mesmerized by the sea of blue that was being televised from inside of New York City's Madison Square Garden.

"Twelve hundred fifty new officers will hit the streets on Monday after six grueling months in the police academy," the newscaster informed, breaking down the boroughs to which they would be apportioned.

The piece ended with a rather simplistic Mother Goose-like quote from the valedictorian's speech: *"We took an oath not knowing how much our lives would change. We leave with the understanding that they will never be the same."*

Giselle actually enjoyed the story, as Greer and Puff angrily ordered her to change the channel, their disdain for the badge-wearing "pigs" supremely evident. They weren't upset about police brutality or the perceived targeting of blacks and other minorities by the NYPD. No, cops interfered with their illegal chosen profession so they were, of course, the natural enemy. I had always wondered if the gangster in a movie knew he or she was the villain—these guys certainly thought the cops were the bad ones. And this was still roughly eight years before individuals with criminal records were killed in police custody—while resisting arrest for breaking laws that elected officials wrote—and martyred by the media, giving birth to a movement. Before new saints were unwittingly created in St. Louis and Staten Island and Baltimore by flawed men and women of the shield. Men and women who had to make split second decisions, as their safety hung precariously in the changing wind, its correctness to be judged by all of America from their cozy, cushiony sofas; their erudite editorials delivered 140 characters at a time, via a bird's chirp.

Giselle did not share the outright disdain for cops that Greer and Puff did. In fact, she was actually attracted to the uncontrived cat and mouse game and often fantasized about being apprehended by a police officer.

"I hope they at least send some sexy ones this time. Not those fat Dunkin Donuts-eating *mofos* who can't even get out of the cars without having a heart attack," she intellectualized, much to the discontent of the drug dealing duo.

"Those fucking swines better keep their snouts the fuck outta' our business. They try to make their quotas off me and Jeff and it's gonna be *ten-the fuck-thirteen*: police officer down," Puff boasted, as he fondled a black 9mm firearm, choking the handle and training the weapon on the television screen.

"Man, fuck the fucking police," Jeff alliterated, his mind somewhat manacled and not exactly by the *Hedera* vines of certain learning institutions that he assuredly was a candidate for. Giselle attached to his statement like a perennial, delivering the type of taboo turn of phrase that this forbidden little cherry would soon become known for.

"Fuck the police?" she verified coquettishly. "State when and where."

This petite paradox of a person—the equivalent of a piece of ice on fire—sat there and licked her passion-filled lips and playfully twitched her eyebrows and oozed sexuality out of her pores without regret or remorse. She was youth's ignorance and arrogance combined together in a pot with magnetism, sass, and scars that made her even more . . . likeable. She hadn't yet encountered Rose but she had certainly visualized him in her self-indulgent ceiling-staring fantasies. Sometimes, young girls don't even know how attractive they are. They can stop the world from spinning if they just styled their hair properly but they're too busy trying to survive to realize that they are gorgeous. Giselle was like that.

The fifty-first precinct muster room smelled like soggy paper, dry cleaning chemicals, and those offensive pharmacy-sold body sprays that teenagers buy. In the full length mirror, Rose examined his line-free face, wondering to himself whether it was a wise idea to have skipped the shaving component of his daily grooming regimen. A sign above the mirror read Self-inspection and Rose went through a visual checklist that included his cap device, collar brass, nameplate, and shield, ensuring that he looked like a blue clad urban soldier with a memorandum pad, known in cop vernacular as a "memo book." Rose inconspicuously looked around at the forty-nine other officers in the room; their crisply-pressed uniforms, their anxious faces, all the gold colored "51s" on their collars proudly proclaiming which precinct they patrol. He gave himself one last glance and nodded his head as if to say "I'm ready." And then Cheddar conducted a visual inspection of his own:

"How'd you get those pants to fit your ass so perfectly? You had them taken in or something?" he inquired, weaving suggestive flamboyance into his kinesics. As something resembling a smile crept across Rose's face, someone resembling a bull burst into the muster room.

Lieutenant Garret was the platoon commander for all the "Operation Impact" rookies and he commanded respect just by breathing in a room. He was tall, intimidating, Italian; the numerous medals that were pinned to his stark white shirt, above his gleaming gold shield, spoke to his hall of fame dossier. He immediately shrank the wooden podium from which he spoke and he threatened to break it simply by leaning on it as he addressed the *kids*:

"Listen up! The color of the day is green. The return date for c summonses is . . . *ah*, the desk officer didn't give it to me. But screw it.

Don't write anybody a summons tonight. Throw the handcuffs on anyone committing a violation and bring them in for a warrant check."

Rose's eyes widened at this and he looked to Cheddar for a reaction. Cheddar blew Rose a kiss and pretended to be writing Garret's words of wisdom in his memo book with a still-capped pen.

Garret continued, "The Dow Jones and my 401(k) are in the shit bowl, but our *COMPSTAT* numbers are through the freaking roof. Up in burglaries, up in rapes, up *seventy-five* percent in homicides; we're getting our asses kicked! We got a robbery pattern going on for months now that's got the detectives scratching their heads when they aren't scratching their balls. You however, cannot afford to scratch your balls. It's baptism by fire here. And if you're afraid to put your hands on *perps*, you can go flip some hamburger at McDonald's."

The lieutenant's speech didn't necessarily inspire anyone on that cold night. Rose certainly wasn't afraid to put his hands on anyone that warranted it and he would prove it fairly early on in his tempestuous career.

Back at 711 Fairplace Avenue, Giselle was rhythmically gyrating her hips in the chilly vestibule as the boys and girls of the fifty-first precinct were getting ready to take to the wintry, mostly abandoned streets. Jeff and Puff were dividing bags of their poisonous product between them and giving Giselle the code word, which she would yell whenever officers approached. It would evidently be "happy new year" on this day.

"Happy new year, you got that, Giselle?" Puff rehearsed with great focus.

"Duh, it's not a fucking sudoku," Giselle offered, displaying her sass and wit, two of her intrinsic companions.

At the precinct, a short, pudgy, lightly-goateed female sergeant— implications of her being a lesbian swirling vigorously through the precinct's gossip channels—stepped to the podium to address the officers. Sergeant Valdez reminded the rookies that some of the undesirables they would likely encounter have diseases and therefore needed to be handled carefully.

"Good evening. In case you haven't realized it, this isn't Beverly Hills. People are poor here, which means they're sick: HIV, TB, Hep C . . . they have the whole alphabet of diseases and you don't want to be taking that crap home to your loved ones," she warned, scanning the crowd with her icy gray eyes.

Lieutenant Garret sliced in and unceremoniously beheaded her speech. He ordered everybody out of the precinct dictatorially and decreed that they go combat crime on their strategically designated foot posts.

"The job is on the streets," he preached. "Grab your radios, a map of the sector boundaries, and fall out to post. *Sarge*, read out the post numbers."

Valdez read the assignments out while disdainfully dismantling Garret in her mind, still envying the white polyester shirt which he filled imperiously and signified his higher rank.

The rookies spilled out of the precinct like water leaking from a punctured bag. They examined their maps quizzically, some pinwheeling them a few times—from portrait to landscape and back—in an effort to view them as intended by their cartographer. A "you are here" beside a stick figure with a badge illustrated the starting point for their journey into the deep, treacherous Bronx night. As Cheddar began to swagger to post, Detective Jones, chomping a tightly rolled, plump Cuban cigar, dumped a bucket of water on him from up above; the rite of passage ritual intended to haze and humble rookies with a little too much *braggadocio* for the seasoned gumshoe's liking. Jones was salted and peppered, and did not approve of what he saw from the vantage point of his third floor office window from the wet and currently soggy newborn. Cheddar did not approve of the ritual:

"You fucking cock-shaped cigar-smoking faggot! Shouldn't you be trying to solve your first crime, you bearded bitch?" he yelled irately, water dripping from his curled lower lip.

"Gotta look up for airmail *rook'*. Next time it might be a can of paint," Jones alerted, before slamming the window shut and returning to his computer. Officer Fernandez needled Cheddar as he *Bachata'd* past him: "Man, another victim of the squad," he uttered, his Mexican accent exaggerated comically.

"The squad?" Cheddar questioned. "Squad of what? Those old farts couldn't solve a crossword puzzle. They're up there trolling the Internet for bestiality porn hoping a perp magically appears in their cells so they can make some overtime. Fucking hacks."

"So this is the maggotlike existence of a bottom feeding rookie police officer, huh?" questioned a doubly arid Rose.

"Who are you? My narrator?" Cheddar asked, dismissing Rose with a flippant hand gesture.

"No, I was the guy whose ass you were staring at in the mirror. Now, I'm the guy who's *gps-ing* where I need to go. You look like the guy who needs a blow-dryer."

"I don't need a blow-dryer; I need a blowjob. And a dry cleaner. That defective probably urinated in that bucket because he couldn't make it to the bathroom in time. Detective Diapers is gonna get his, you'll see."

The two collaborated on a smile and proceeded to amble off to post in different directions, with different partners on this particular night. They hadn't yet formed their bond or been linked by destiny, as the Ash Wednesday massacre was still just a sketchily conceived plot at this point.

Rose scanned nameplates for his assigned partner, locating Officer Smith and politely introducing himself to her. There, the night softened and the two strolled to post together; their radios loud, the leather of their gun belts rigid and still not broken in. They took in the moment of their first walk to post as law enforcement agents, the aura of it acting as a cushion underneath their heels. They were in awe of and frightened by their powers, still unsure of how to wield them and wondering if the other person was more knowledgeable and less afraid or experiencing the exact same feeling. The eye contact they occasionally made in between surveying each other peeled away their shyness and would unfurl their tightly wrapped personalities. When they arrived to post, they each wrote one sentence in their memorandum pad, cheating a bit by sneaking a look at the other person's pad. In vastly different handwritings they recorded the entry to prove that they were where they needed to be:

"1800 hours: 10-84 on post. No violations observed."

Rose wrote like a female and Smith wrote like a male, if you believe in such gender-based graphological prejudices. It is strange to say, but you can almost tell by Rose's decorative penmanship that he had a vibrance to him, not of someone trying to be noticed, but of someone daring to shine. These two things might appear similar, but they are different in the way being seen and helping others see are distinct. Rose *could* one day light the way. He himself perhaps didn't yet recognize that he possessed this light inside of him which radiated outwardly. But he had to be aware of the flame that crackled inside of him; his ambition to be like his father pouring gasoline on it slowly, consistently, steadily. Smith decided she would try and get to know the young firebrand before he dynamited and his ambitious pursuits rendered him inaccessible.

"I remember you from my gym block in the academy. We did the boxing drill together; do you remember me?"

"I boxed with you in the academy?" Rose doubted.

"Yes! You spent the entire afternoon apologizing."

"Apologizing? That's not ringing a bell right now."

"Actually, you rang *my* bell. Right hook, right through the pads. You caught my nose too."

"Is that why it looks like that?" Rose joked incompatibly, attempting to be charmless.

"No, that's because I'm half Jamaican and half Irish."

Smith gently squeezed at her nose, selling the joke, while opening up her envelope a little bit to Rose. He counted the small constellation of light brown freckles that made her iridescent green eyes even more striking. He acquainted himself with her features, taking a mental photograph of her as she made a bid to endear herself to him by way of her inherent allure and subtle vulnerability. Her outline was quickly becoming a picture to him. Perhaps, subconsciously, this caused him to look down at his cell phone's home screen, which showcased an image of the girl he vowed to always love and come home to. Rose doted on the snapshot of Cecelia, lamenting the fact that she would in actuality not be there if and when he made it home later that morning—it is always if and when with cops. Rose loved her but loathed the distance between them. But he was a prisoner to the situation and inmates often dream of breaking free.

"So, are you going to stare at your phone all night long or are we gonna patrol?" Smith asked, interrupting Rose's divergent thoughts.

Just as he was preparing to reply, a rather tall and slender youth, an African-American male, waddled out of the bodega with pants that hung far below his buttocks, which he appeared to keep up with his thighs. This seemed absurd considering he had a very expensive looking belt, with a garish gold belt buckle completely and properly fastened. The incongruity of this aside, the young man probably would not have been noticed had he not collided into Officer Smith in his haste to make it back to his apartment to roll the Philly Blunt that he had just purchased. The young man scowled back and continued walking.

"Hey! Sir . . . hey, my man, you ever heard of the words 'excuse me'?" Rose growled.

"I'm not your man and she shouldn't have been standing there."

"How about you apologize for bumping into her? Would you bump into your mother and not say anything?" Rose questioned, angering incrementally.

"You rookies are buggin'. If I was a white man would you be talking to me like that? No. You'd be kissing my white ass and apologizing to me. But since I'm black, now it's a fucking problem, like nobody bumps into nobody in the goddamn hood."

"I don't give two shits if you're razzmatazz pink, man. You do not bump into an officer of the law and not apologize. That's *101*. That's manners 101 for any civilized person."

Rose and the young man were now intertwined in an unwinnable argument and were revolving downward like the helix of a barber's pole, each representing a distinct color that could never bleed into the other. Despite Smith's attempt to pull Rose away from the confrontation, it was evident that hubris had a better grip and stronger pull at this precise moment. Rose took his status as a police officer seriously and was taught that if you allow someone to disrespect you while you wear the uniform you just succeeded in making life that much more difficult for the next cop he encounters. What he heard next took negotiating off the table.

"Fuck you, you fucking pig. Leave me alone so I can go home and smoke my blunt!"

"Fuck you and your blunt," Rose retaliated. "Give me your I.D. card, you're getting a summons."

"A summons for what? Being black? Come on my *nigga'* there's freedom of speech in this country, remember that?"

"I am not your *nigga'* and you are causing public alarm, so hand over your I.D. before I put my foot in your black ass."

In an instant, Rose had gone somewhere he never intended to go. He was like a virtuous pinwheel being blown by sinful winds. He was spiraling, cartwheeling toward something he detested. From the very pit of his soul to the peak of his idealistic, maverick mind he wanted to believe that racism did not exist. He knew better, of course, but he believed he was immune from looking down at someone because of their physical traits.

When the young man took his middle finger and stuck it directly in between Rose's eyes—about an inch from his nose—Rose may have whispered a racial epithet under his breath in the heat of the moment. Nobody heard it, but Rose knew it. Upon moving in to grab the youngster, Rose was shoved joltingly and a wrestling match ensued. Smith imitated the water in an ice tray as Rose propelled the dissentient over his head into a metal wire trash receptacle close by. This was a sight to behold as the young man sailed head first into the garbage and some of New York City's unwanted treasures spilled out.

"You're under arrest, you fucking mutt!" Rose bellowed as he applied the handcuffs. Smith opened her plump, pink lips to her radio's speaker microphone but was unclear of what to transmit.

"Smith, get the address off the damn sign and let Central know we have a collar," Rose ordered.

"Five-one posts five and six, Central, show us with one under from the corner of . . . Harmony Avenue and Tremont. Can you please have the patrol supervisor respond?"

Lieutenant Garret had been traveling around the South Bronx in an all-black, completely tinted Chevrolet Impala. He heard the transmission and began making his way to the scene of the incident. When he arrived, both officers tendered crisp salutes to their imposing boss.

"What'd you get him for?" asked the platoon commander.

"He shoved me, sir. He was very belligerent, disrespectful. I asked him for his I.D. . . ."

"To hell with him, assault on a police officer," Garret interjected. "Let the ADA lower the charge, if anything. This sack of shit needs to learn. Are you taking it?"

Smith suddenly got the urge to speak up: "Rose, you mind if I take it? I'm very anxious to get my first collar and I think this would be a good one for me since I witnessed everything."

Rose's face scrunched up in disbelief and he was on the verge of having his first arrest politely stolen from him after exerting so much energy and emotion in his first ever street encounter in uniform. He placed the arrestee in the back of Garret's car and presented his book for the lieutenant to sign. The lieutenant examined the second generation cop's uniform and scribbled in Rose's memo book.

"1830 hours: Lieutenant Garret visited c/o Harmony and East Tremont, N/V/O."

When Rose received his memo book back, he was also unanticipatedly smacked with a brusque question.

"Rose, huh? That's a good name on this job—strong. You don't happen to be related to a certain first grade detective, do you?"

Rose could feel his eyes begin to lubricate. A faint chill ran up his spine and the hair on his arms stood up like wind-blown grass. He poker-faced his way through the impromptu interrogation, barely managing a soft no.

"Oh. . . All right. It's just that you look like this guy, you remind me of him. Damn that guy was good. Detective Rose, he was an old partner of mine for a brief time."

Rose just chewed on his upper lip and stared at the tips of his creased work boots. He prayed the lieutenant would just about-face into his vehicle and drive off, taking the emotion he just evoked away in the back seat of the sedan like a perpetrator.

"Just meet up with this kid Fuchetti over at Fairplace Avenue," Garret read from a curling roster. "His partner just got a nice little *pinch* out of that cesspool. Maybe you guys can collar up too and get on the sheet early."

"Yes, sir. I'll try and get you something good tonight," Rose calculated, casually kissing up while steadying his slightly trembling voice.

"That's what I'm talking about! Ah, quotas. I fucking love them," the lieutenant revealed, practically salivating.

The lieutenant and Smith and her penitent prisoner drove away in that black Impala through the angular shadows and artificial light of the night. Rose made his way over to Fairplace as the weight of his gun belt began to take its toll on his gait—which was evolving into a full-out waddle—and he replayed his first encounter over and over again, refrigerating it in a cool compartment of his mind. The memory would remain fresh and Rose would snack on it often.

Later that night, Rose walked up to Cheddar in front of the building numbered 711 Fairplace, and together they stepped into an unacknowledged partnership. Awkward silence and the wintry chill, both present in the air, possessed much better chemistry than them at this primitive point. Cheddar stared at Rose's immaculate uniform, comparing it to his own inferior, sauce-stained equivalent.

"The '*lieu*' said I gotta partner up with you," Rose relayed, insinuating in his tone that he would never arrive at such a determination himself.

"Is that right?" Cheddar asked, before raising his right leg off the ground and angling its connected gluteals moonward.

"FRRRAP!"

In one fell swoop, Cheddar had given Rose insight into his etiquette, broken the ice to commence interaction, and tested his ability to contract his anus in a timely fashion. Rose clung to a serious face before surrendering to childish laughter and waving his hand through the air to help dissipate the sound's accompanying stench. The two laughed in synchrony and extended their communal moment by intermittently cackling every time silence was achieved. It was goofy and infantile but it was a moment they needed.

As the two officers guffawed the night away, a beer can was making its way across a room within the building; tumbling through the air until its path was abruptly interrupted, cracking against Giselle's comely face.

"You've got the easiest job in the world and you fuck it up?" Puff complained, kicking the beer can after the brutal ricochet. "We pay you to look out, you little slore!"

"*Slore?*" Giselle disputed, caressing her eye gently, taking extra care to ensure she didn't wipe away the skillfully applied makeup.

"Slore: half slut, half whore. How come you left without telling us? That was a good customer that got pinched," he assessed before Greer tagged himself in and made the verbal beat down a two on one affair.

"These pigs are everywhere. If motherfuckers start getting locked up when they come to buy, we ain't gonna make no paper, *Gizzy*. Come on, bitch!"

"What about my paper? You still haven't paid me for last week," Giselle reminded. "I miss school for this shit. I don't do my homework for this shit."

"Bitch, this is your homework. School is out. Making bread is in. You gon' get paid for last week but if you fuck up again, I'm gonna smack those dick sucking lips of yours right off your pretty face."

Puff mechanically nodded his head in agreement and went back to packaging the bags of dope that he would later sell to local junkies, known as *methadonians* or "zombies." Giselle scraped her self-worth off the floor and exited the apartment, chin tucked into her chest, as her pride and dignity further bruised at the hands of her two horrid handlers.

At the precinct, inside the holding pens, Fernandez examined Smith's shapely silhouette.

"Damn, girl. I'm gonna tell Sarge to make us partners. I wanna be your *personal* training officer," he detailed, carefully taking in every curve of her figure eight physique. "I'll get you mad collars. You'll make so much overtime, you'll bring new meaning to the phrase 'collars for dollars'."

Smith pointed to an addict, involuntarily bobbing and weaving in the cells, still under the control of the magic rock.

"Collars for dollars, huh? Are you sure it isn't more like cash for trash?"

Sometimes in life, worlds collide. It happens so innocuously that you don't even realize the beautiful pieces of wreckage that ballet through the air, post-impact. As Rose and Cheddar were growing more familiar with one another, Giselle was reacquainting herself with a makeup brush, which she used to apply splashes of shimmery pink blush to that unforgettable face. She darkened her mascara and curved her eyeliner up exotically at the outer corners in an effort to conceal her newly negotiated black eye. She pulled a well-traveled twenty-dollar bill from out of her sky blue push up bra and darted across the street like a colorful streak of trouble. In that moment, heat met danger and Giselle was struck by a splashy red convertible, which was blasting rap music at hyperbolic noise levels. The smell of rubber burned in the frosty air as the car screaked off in reverse just as Rose and Cheddar came stampeding in. Rose dropped to his knees and delicately put his fingers to her tiny wrist, sliding her eclectic silver charm bracelet up, feeling for a pulse. And boy was there a throbbing coming from her veins. Yes, she was alive and relatively well with a heart that was about to pound in a distinctly different manner than it had ever beat before.

"Hey! Little girl, can you hear me?" Rose asked, speaking into her dainty, bejeweled ears. Cheddar reached for his portable radio, summoning assistance.

"Five-one portable, Central. Show me with a pickup of a pedestrian struck in front of 711 Fairplace Avenue. The motorist fled the scene in a red convertible, which turned right onto Croton Avenue. Rush a bus over here *forthwith!*"

Rose framed her face with his palms and shook her head the way you shake a box to determine what kind of gift is inside it, but as if her head had a Fragile sticker across it.

"Little girl! Can you hear me? What's your name, what's today's date?" Rose asked frenetically, just as Giselle was unveiling those gigantic orbs that are supposed to pass for eyes but might as well be planets. Rose brushed a grouping of rich locks away from her face and Giselle instantly captured him in the net of her gaze. All of her alluring teenage features were now revealed as Rose's face lowered by the natural pull of gravity and possibly chemistry. Giselle smiled. Rose half-smiled. Neither spoke. Splashes of color and glitter glistened as Giselle traced a face she found so intriguing. She memorized the shape of his eyes and the slope of his nose. She followed the direction of his hair and recorded the warm beige of his Caribbean skin tone.

"Who are you calling 'little girl'?" she protested. "And today is July 10th, 1776. *Duh!*"

"Cheddar, she's a little banged up," Rose determined. "She probably has a concussion or something. Put a rush on that bus, man."

"Man, I don't need no bus! I'm fine," she declared. "And that's the day Congress appointed a committee of five to draft the Declaration of Independence. They teach you history in the academy, no?"

Rose quizzically stared at his newfound friend. He couldn't quite decipher if she was acting or if she actually was crazy.

"Cheddar, you think she's *EDP?*"

"What? You think I'm emotionally disturbed? I'm not a nut job, I'm a history buff," she explained.

"Oh really, *buffy?* Okay, I take it back. Now, are you sure you're okay? Because if that car would have hit you any harder you'd be in Manhattan right now."

"Well, it beats the bullshit Bronx," she quipped, giving a glimpse into the capabilities of her endearing, vulgar mouth.

"Show me by pointing where you feel the pain," Rose requested, taking in her petite body.

Giselle remained on the ground and pointed to the left side of her chest before outlining the shape of a heart with her index finger.

"Right here is where it hurts. Broken heart. Incapable of being repaired. *Mi corazoncito* will never heal."

Rose found the theatrics humorous and he extended both of his arms to her but she persisted on the ground, her stage now, dramatizing her injury.

"You really can't move, Juliet?"

"No, Romeo, I'm paralyzed," she rebutted, before disproving that by flailing her arms and legs as if she were making a snow angel with the one problematic element being the absence of any snow.

"Why are we waiting for a 'bus'—an ambulance—when you can call one of the old geezers in an RMP and they can take me."

"'*RMP*'? Most people say squad car or patrol car," Rose noted accurately.

"Well, I'm not most people. I'm Giselle Elizabeth Ignacio."

"Woah, slow down there. That's a lot of vowels. I didn't get all that."

"Giselle, like the supermodel. Elizabeth, like the Queen of England. Ignacio, like the saint."

Her introduction announced a confidence that contradicted her permanently fractured self-esteem. But she was putting on a show for Rose, and he sat captive in his orchestra seat giving her credibility for reasons not yet known. Rose appeared to be temporarily incapacitated, like an insect caught in a spider's web. He languished in her silk net, moving neither to his left nor to his right as she began to sink her fangs into him. She stood up and stepped closer to him, her little segmented body moving by two alternating tagmata: her pushup bra-enhanced breasts which dominated her torso, and an uncommonly large, bulbous derriere, which bounced left to right like a pinball caught in between two bumpers. She controlled the tempo.

"Usually, when one person says who they are, the other person says who *they* are. That's called an introduction," she explained in a childish whisper that disguised the adult game she was playing.

"How rude of me. I'm Derek Jeter," Rose revealed kiddingly, partaking of her sport.

"You look different in person, *Jetes'.*"

"It's because I'm wearing a different cap."

"Whatever you say, *cap'*," she cracked from her whip smart muzzle.

Cheddar was growing uncomfortable at this point. He interrupted the verbal volley, in essence turning a glacier into crushed ice for cocktails.

"Hey, Rose, after you and this slab of jail bait are done exchanging saliva, you might want to write her name, date of birth, and address on this here *police accident report*. You know, the one you gotta fill out, because you're *working*?" Like a bull in ballet slippers, Cheddar delicately tiptoed around what was transpiring.

"Thank you, A-Rod. I can always count on the third baseman to slit my throat," Rose replied with equal subtlety.

"Okay, Giselle," Rose prepped, holding a black ballpoint pen in between his fingers. "What were you doing right before you got hit by that vehicle?"

"Are you sure you can handle it?"

Rose affirmed yes via an exaggerated head nod and so she proceeded.

"I was looking out, for these drug dealing scumbags. Who smack me around whenever the hell they please, I might add. Earlier tonight, I forgot to tip them off that you boys were around and your partner over here had a different partner who collared some junkie. So yeah, I fucked up . . ."

"Hey! Just the facts, ma'am," Rose demanded.

"Those are the facts. Excuse the potty mouth but if you've seen the shit I've seen you'd be gargling crap in the morning instead of Listerine."

Rose turned to Cheddar who shrugged and did a little symphony conductor's wave as if to say "it's your show, maestro."

"So, you're telling me you're the reason that the officer made a collar— excuse me—an *arrest* earlier tonight? Because you didn't properly perform your duties of being a lookout for the drug dealers? Am I correct in saying this?"

"I'm just one of numerous players on this block. My alias? Roger Sherman."

"Who in the blue hell is Roger Sherman?" inquired Rose, unaware that he was about to receive an impromptu lesson in syndicate hierarchy and American History.

"*Sssh*, try and keep up with me. In this outfit, there are five of us. *D* is Thomas Jefferson, the big dog, leader of the pack. He is our architect just like the Founding Father who drew up the blueprint known as the Declaration of Independence. *K*, his number one, is Bejamin Franklin, the money man. He's solid at everything but mainly he counts . . . the Benjamins, get it? *P* is John Adams, the *vice president*. He's pretty much second to D but does a lot of dirty work on the streets, so he's at a different location. Then there's *J*. He's Robert Livingston and a real piece of shit. He's known as *The Chancellor* because he fashions himself as some type of bullshit street lawyer. In case you're wondering, I made up the names. The four of them together couldn't get an academic multiple choice question right if they each chose a different letter . . . and there's no '*e*' option," Giselle concluded, all but taking a bow.

Rose grinned at all this, reflected right back at him by an even bigger twinkling grin. Unfriendly faces watched, partly obstructed, through curtains and venetian blinds at this most atypical interaction.

"I get it now: you and your constituents run the cartel and your self-given *nom de guerre* is Robert Sherman?"

"*Roger* Sherman. And maybe it's a *nom de plume*. Did I help draft the document? I don't know. Do I look out for the Smurfs, so my boys can sell their product in peace? You damn right. If you get to know me really well, you can just call me *G*," Giselle offered, tilting her head flirtatiously while hiding behind extremely long eye lashes that curled up toward the dematerialized sun.

"I'm trying to figure out why you're telling me this," Rose vocalized, curling his body down into her. "You literally just met me. I can detain you for this. And the last time I checked snitches get stitches out here."

"What are stitches to a girl who's already in pieces? What are they gonna do? Glue me back together so they can slice me open and then stitch me up again?"

Rose did not understand how she could simultaneously be so damaged and yet so pristine. She had been emotionally mutilated by the predators whom she worked for, but yet she had a cerebral fortitude which appeared indestructible. To think of Giselle as someone shattered stood in direct opposition to the shatterproof girl who stood before Rose at this moment.

"Is this your cry for help?"

"No, Sigmund Freud. This is not. Why, does my sob story make you want to save me? Save my little Latina life?"

"I save people who need saving," Rose declared with a fervent idealistic sincerity that is not connate in all police officers.

"You wanna save this poor child?" Giselle pressed. "Save me from the mean streets and the wolf pack and becoming a statistic?"

"I'm a police officer. If you need to be saved I will save you," Rose underscored genuinely.

Before anything had truly been settled, an ambulance rumbled up and two EMS workers treated the young minx. They placed a neck brace on her and loaded her onto an ambulance cot. Giselle embraced the attention, turning up the volume on the dramatics. She winked at Rose and he rolled his eyes to the back of his head in return. She stuck out her pointy, wet tongue as he shook his head disapprovingly, yet somehow still fettered by her imprisoning gaze. She moved her tongue in the most non-virginal way and the leverage of this was resignedly noticed, and properly unacknowledged, by the adults in her path.

"Rose! I never got your first name?" she essentially demanded.

27

"*Officer.* It's Officer Rose."

"Wow, imagine the odds," she marveled, as she consumed him one last time. "Oh, and what about your boyfriend over there? What's his name?" she lobbed from behind a quip.

"Fuchetta! *Fu*, like kung fu. *Cheddar* like the cheese. Everyone calls me Cheddar but you can call me never," Rose's surrogate half-jested with zero amusement for the girl.

"Okay, call you tomorrow you said, right? Is your number still 911 or did you change it again?"

Giselle asked this through the teeth of a smile as big as the compartment of the ambulance into which she was being wheeled. The ambulance doors slammed shut. Rose and Cheddar proceeded to lean on the scorched hood of a derelict vehicle and fill out the police accident report unassuredly—like an infant taking its first steps. . . in quicksand.

"What in the hell just happened?" Cheddar queried, annoyance discernible in his rhythmic, accented voice.

"I don't know, but I think that little girl just told us she could be our confidential informant," rejoiced Rose, a celebratory dance permeating his body movements.

"Bullshit, man. You can't have a C.I. Plus, she's underage. The department will ass-rape you. The commissioner will personally take his tree trunk-like dick and impale you. His penis will be the skewer and you'll be a kebab," metaphorized Cheddar, pantomiming penetration with his masculine fist.

"You're having a little too much fun with that analogy," Rose replied with a smile, partially enjoying the comparison himself. "But listen, my dad had a C.I. That's actually how he made detective. This hobo would tip him off and lead him to all types of drug collars, gun collars. I'm talking major busts. He used him all the way until he made grade."

"Your dad? Oh, so you're a blue blood, huh? You're police royalty with an elite pedigree? Figures. And did your dad's informant have peach fuzz on her teenage vagina?"

"Wow, you are dirty, dog. But why are you imagining her *thing* though?"

"You know you probably pictured it," Cheddar returned, "stop acting like you're Pope John Paul the fifth or something."

"You're a pervert. Do you know that?" an appalled Rose posed." Not only are you going to hell but you're going to walk a foot post for twenty years before you go there. Meanwhile, I'll be a detective telling you to hold my coffee while I examine a crime scene, collecting evidence which I will make you voucher, my son."

"You ain't getting no gold shield, Inspector Gadget. You're rookie slime. You making detective is a pipe dream."

"So then let me dream, my man. We're in America, land of opportunity, no? Bronx, New York: murder capital of the world. This place needs more detectives to solve all these goddamn homicides. It might as well be me."

Rose declared this, in the process unmasking the enthusiast who was pushing his idealistic desire to climb, perhaps prematurely, within the department. He was a striver, unembarrassed, and he looked down on Cheddar for his actionless satisfaction with merely being a grunt on a street corner. Rose and Cheddar continued to enjoy the quasi-hostile banter which was, in actuality, bonding them. As their pace intensified, the verbal combatants were parted by the referee in the form of an EMT.

"Excuse me, fellas, our *aided* is only sixteen. One of you is going to have to ride with us and stay at the hospital until a parent shows up."

"Hold up, we have to go to the hospital with medusa?" Cheddar pushed back, while gently shoving Rose in the direction of the ambulance, summarily volunteering his partner for the assignment.

"Does she even have parents?" begged Rose.

"Well, that's the thing. She told us she was raised by wolves. A wolf pack she said."

"Let me guess," attempted Rose, "they happen to be former U.S. presidents?"

Rose informed Cheddar that he would ride in the rear compartment and so he pulled opened the doors, revealing the black sunshine that was Giselle.

"So I guess you have to stay and babysit the problem child? I love it when a plan comes together," she gloated, kicking her feet up and down like a swimmer.

Giselle's face lit up at the sight of Rose like when they flip the switch at Rockefeller Center. Emotions skated across her face as she smiled and her eyes glistened and her lips shimmered with their raspberry lip gloss sending subtle aromas into the space that enclosed them. Her face blushed, pomegranate seed-like, and she danced with excitement on the stretcher that suddenly felt like an amusement park ride. Rose grabbed the seatbelt and fastened her in, clicking it and tugging at it to ensure Giselle was secure. He jerked the strap, further tightening it, in the process bringing his body overly close to hers. She leaned into this opportunistically, hoping a speed bump in the yet stationary ambulance would deposit Rose onto the stretcher with her. Rose sat himself down on the transport bench and took out his cell phone to photograph his willing subject.

"I have to photograph the injured. It's protocol."

"Don't be putting that shit on Facebook," she warned.

"It's for America's Most Wanted," he joked, as the EMS paramedic once again slammed the doors shut and commenced the bumpy trip to the hospital. Rose and Giselle, by some odd twist of fate, were now obligated to get to know each other better. Giselle shone gloriously in this newly-birthed opportunity—one that she twistedly, but perhaps not inaccurately, perceived as an audition for something greater further on in their relationship.

I didn't know it then, but when Giselle collided with that 1971 red Corvette Stingray Convertible, she did so much more than just deflect off of a car. She was actually rocketed out of her self-gravitating world— Giselle's world—and onto the shores of Rose's vastly dissimilar planet. Rose ran in so quickly after hearing the thud that he practically stepped on the precocious teenager, almost crushing her pint-sized body in the process. Some might consider this destiny—I certainly did. After all, why would God place two people within inches of each other, so theatrically at that, without a purpose? No one knew that purpose yet. It still seemed mostly innocuous at this point, like a transparent nail polish that didn't actually change the color of anything, only glossed over what was already there. But it appeared the change was coming.

At the hospital, Rose went above and beyond. He fed Giselle applesauce and massaged her head, which was plagued by a mild headache, perhaps more plaguing now that adrenaline and the excitement of her initial meeting with Rose had subsided into more of a blanket-like comfort. A nurse entered, interrupting whatever organic thing was developing between them.

"Okay, she's medically cleared. No broken bones. Have you been able to contact a parent or guardian yet, officer?" the nurse asked Rose, who experienced no such contemplation.

"I don't have parents or guardians, nurse. I'm an emancipated child," Giselle angrily corrected.

"You can't be emancipated. Because the paperwork I have for you says you're sixteen. You can't be emancipated until you're seventeen. And you can't leave the hospital until we get in touch with a parent or guardian."

This reiteration angered Giselle. Her up until now sweet, childlike voice climbed in pitch.

"So I guess I'm never leaving this hospital because my dad was shot and killed by a rival gang member before I was even born and my mom committed suicide *after* I was born. Are you really gonna keep me here because I'm a bastard child? And if so I hope you have a year's supply of tampons, tube socks, and toothpaste because a young lady absolutely cannot have her *cooch*, toes, or breath smelling like a bum's nut sack in the year 2007. It's highly impertinent."

"Nurse, do you have services available?" Rose rescued. "I mean, someone to care for her in place of parents?"

"Services?" Giselle repeated angrily. "I don't need *services*. ACS will come and scoop me right up as soon as you process me and I'm released from the bookings."

"Bookings?" Rose parroted, perplexed.

"Well, I *am* under arrest, remember?"

Giselle pulled a small plastic bag of marijuana out from a pocket of her jeans, which were neatly folded in a transparent hospital bag. "Unless you wanna keep this bag of *ganja* our little secret," she hissed, ahead of a victorious wink that left Rose flat-footed.

"Officer, if she's under arrest she can go. I don't need to hold her. She's in your custody."

"Yeah, I'm in your custody. Did you hear that? Let's go."

The nurse looked over Giselle, who was placing her hands behind her back tauntingly. Rose waved off handcuffing her and instead helped her gather her belongings. Giselle went into the bathroom and changed out of the hospital gown and back into her own clothes. Rose and his little reclamation project from the projects exited the hospital, their time together once again lengthened by Giselle's swift thinking.

In a back alley, converging shadows overwhelmed the waning artificial light, which was barely managing a fight, and Giselle explained to Rose how she was brought up by neighborhood drug dealers and how she sleeps in a child-size room at 711 Fairplace. She made an unbidden promise to him that when she turned seventeen she would retire from the only job she had ever held.

"I better not catch you looking out for those drug dealing scumbags again," Rose followed up. "And once you turn seventeen you know what that means, right? It means you can get locked up like an adult: big girl prison."

"You know what it means to me? It means we can date!" Giselle countered optimistically.

Rose waved his finger rejectingly and eased away into the starless night, its purple sky in sedated motion from the overlying cloud cover. Giselle stood directly in the center of a singular square of the night-chilled pavement, waiting for a hug that never materialized. The only thing that embraced her there was a conservative wind and then a crippled street lamp offered to warm her from high atop, in the process illuminating her rather cinematically. In a moment, under the light, she was already reminiscing on the night, which was concurrently vivid and hazy like a Renoir painting. She knew that she had just been impacted by a man, in some way, and she knew that she wanted to gain purchase on his heart, which she viewed as ripe for her picking.

Still, she let Rose stroll away further into the night, like the silhouettes in Munch's *The Scream,* but ambling away from her, not pursuing her—she wished that was the case. She wanted to perform something like a scream as the colors swirled in her suddenly changed world, revealing to her that sometimes the landscape does indeed shift. Giselle squealed in excitement. That was her great eruption that night. And the first of various times that Rose would melt the oft icy girl and leave without mopping up the puddle.

But Rose made one grave mistake: turning back to her as he walked away. He gave the obligatory wave and then her *come here* eyes—her secret weapon—went to work on him, systematically. He wasn't precisely sure of what to make of those half-concealed, partially mysterious glances which she shot at him like honeyed javelins. But they appeared to paralyze him momentarily as they emanated from behind the panes of incandescent eyes. That led Rose to believe that perhaps her heart was catching fire. And for this blaze he had no water but, evidently, gasoline was abundant and they were standing on the precipice of combustion.

Rose left her there, and sluggishly rode the vagabond-carrying number one train home that night, allowing the sizzling heat of their first encounter to subside into the cooler temperature of subterranean New York City train travel. He dozed off and then dashed out precisely before the doors closed on the night chill—and his broad back—at the elevated 231st street station which, until he could advance his career, was still his stop.

Chapter III

By the time Rose made it back to his apartment early that morning, he barely possessed the energy required to open up the leather-bound edition of the King James Bible resting at his nightstand—which was adorned with interlaced cup ring marks left behind by cheap sparkling wine. Rose returned to his last page, designated by a gold-tipped, hollow point 9mm round, which preserved the reading: "Then was Jesus led up of the spirit into the wilderness to be tempted of the devil . . ." Just as he was about to dive spiritually into Matthew, a melodic ring tone emitted from his cell phone. An angelic voice met his greeting, filling Rose with champagne-like bubbles in his stomach.

"My love, were you sleeping?" Cecelia asked with the gentleness of a cotton ball. It was Cecelia who brought the music into his life. Rose fell in love with her voice at that moment; the exact key in which she spoke was so pleasing to his ears. He cleared his throat and transferred his muddled thoughts into words.

"No baby, I was just about to do some reading. I thought about calling you, but I figured it was already past twelve in San Francisco, right? I'm still trying to get the whole time difference thing dow—"

"It's simple, my love," she politely interrupted, "we're just three hours behind New York. When you get home around three in the morning, it's midnight over here. And I'm up reading the Bible, like we used to do before we went to sleep. And I'm just waiting for my sweetheart's call."

Cecelia stated this with tears streaming down the pleasing topography of her face. Rose twirled a bullet in between his fingers and imagined that face, somehow missing the cues in her voice to intimate that she was crying. The fiancés revealed how much they missed each other and how badly they longed to hold one another, as distance and time hunkered down in the gulf that separated them, preparing to make nights like these their agonizing norm.

"Did you make any arrests today?" Cecelia asked through light sniffles.

"Sort of. Somebody else took it. But really I did all the work. Someone got hit by a car on my post though, which turned out pretty interesting," Rose volunteered, in essence saying too much.

"Oh no! That's horrible. Are they okay?"

"Yeah, she was fine. It was some girl—a teenager—her name was *Giselle*," he divulged, adding an eminence to the pronunciation that Cecelia did not overlook. "She was something else."

"What do you mean by *something else*? Was she memorable to you?" demanded Cecelia, her female intuition now steering her focused inquisitiveness.

"No, no, no," Rose defended. "She was just . . . she was a hood rat basically, but with a really smart mouth. She was very persistent and would make these humorous remarks, that's all."

Rose understood that Cecelia was dissecting every word he said, not out of insecurity but due to the natural disadvantage that she was faced with by simply not being in New York with him.

"Listen, there's no need to go on about this street urchin. I want to talk about my regal, radiant, *ravishing* fiancée and figure out exactly when I can see her precious face again."

The lovers loved each other over the phone. It was a consolation prize they would often unwrap. This was their life now: repetitions and reversals hampered by the natural laws of space and its destructive companion—separation. Their eyelids got heavy and they exchanged fading I-love-yous. The pair slowly drifted off into the realm of dream and neither would remember where the conversation concluded the following day. Rose's subconscious floated him past a chain of smoking, sweating hotdog carts and their vibrant umbrellas and onto the glossy hardwood floor of the world-famous Madison Square Garden.

Applauses thundered, confetti drizzled down, and stark white dress gloves hailed from as high up as the four hundred level after being tossed skyward as a celebratory ritual by recruits who had just graduated from the police academy. This took place amidst the backdrop of retired basketball and hockey jerseys hanging from the rafters as Rose scanned the crowd—an impressionist painter's polychromatic rendition in this dream—for the faces of those whom he loved. Rose cut short the embraces from the newly-minted officers who congratulated him as he attempted to locate his mother and fiancée. In his dream these two women, so vital to his being, looked similar to one another and not exactly as they do in real life. They were *gestalts* of themselves, closer to sketches or ideas which informed him that they indeed were the two most beloved women in his life. Rose cried outwardly in this vision, as he could not secure their attention, and they appeared to pierce right through him with their eyes as they too searched for him in vain. A seat next to them was initially vacant; then the tears in Rose's eyes somehow produced a magnifying effect which, when brought completely into focus, revealed that someone was in fact there.

It was then that Rose's father, Detective First Grade Reinaldo Rose, materialized into that space. He was clad in his pristine blue dress uniform decorated by a glossy, gold detective's shield: a dodecagon with a small rectangular border under it housing the numbers 1004. The geometric lines around the inner, circular, blue part of the badge emanated out like unvarying rays of the sun's light, every sixth line jutting out like the spire atop the Empire State Building. The shield glistened, its immense glare blocking out Rose's view of his father's chiseled chin and well-defined face. Rose swam through the audience, his uniform staining from the kaleidoscopic blemishes of the oil paint, which comprised the throng. When he arrived at his father's seat he leaned in, eyes closed, to hug his hero. Merely a restless draft returned embrace and then a gold shield fell to the ground, *clinking* loudly as it hit, far too amplified to be real. A crestfallen Rose wept in an empty arena as a church hymn was played from an invisible organ. Rose clutched a Bible, which appeared from out of the thin air of his impressionist-surrealist imagining, and squeezed it to his chest.

"I will trust in him. I will trust in him," Rose repeated as he was jettisoned from his sleep and thrust into the popcorn ceiling of his apartment, stalactite-like pieces crunching off and crumbling onto his head. Sweat baked him and chilled him simultaneously as he interpreted his surroundings. Rose swept at his covers, cloaking himself in whatever fabric he could gather up as he tried to reacquaint himself with reality and separate himself from the desolation of his dream. When Rose finally acclimated, he bunched up his sweat-soaked covers and stuffed them into a wicker clothes hamper. He ruffled his hair, smacked his own face and reached for his Bible, which opened up to a verse about ashes and dust. He reverentially placed the holy book down on his nightstand and checked his wall calendar. It read:

"Wednesday, February 21st, 2007 – Ash Wednesday *Go to church and get ashes."

Rose introspected and he looked out of his window at the barren trees of February, devoid of life and color. He looked in the mirror at one day old stubble and puffy eyes, soiled by dried-up crust at the corners, and he wondered to himself how in the living hell two months had passed by in a single psychedelic night of sleep. He pieced together tokens of reality to confirm his consciousness, feeling for mundane walls to affirm that he was back in the boring terrestrial realm.

On the afternoon of that first day of Lent, with the air heavy—not with spirituality or repentance but with the menacing specter of tragedy looming predatorily over the night—Officers Rose, Smith, Hernandez, and a few others waited in line, in full NYPD regalia, to receive their ashes at a small, broken Catholic church along their foot post. Once Rose crisscrossed the universal sign of Jesus' sacrifice over his forehead, lips, and heart he soldiered over to his assigned area of the Bronx to perform what he truly felt at his core was God's work. There, he was intercepted by a sixteen-year-old bottle rocket wearing a mischievous smile and eyes that devour. She flipped her ample mane sexily over to the other side of her head, looking tousled and talking Bronx tough.

"So, you're back on my block, huh?" Giselle asked with authority. "I thought I was gonna have to put in a special request for you. I was getting tired of watching that trained monkey write parking tickets here."

"You missed me, did you?" Rose suspected. "It *has* been a while. I was hoping you turned seventeen and finally moved out of this wasteland." Rose painted a rosy outlook while trying to make sense of Giselle's scant, inviting attire in the pallid depths of winter.

"Tryna' get rid of me so soon? Remember I gotta keep working until I pay off my college loans."

"Yeah, I'm sure. University of hard knocks, right?"

"Nah, the university of hard co—"

Rose interrupted Giselle by bringing his hand to her mouth and she curled her bottom lip around his thumb and sensually drew it into her sultry hole. She sucked his thumb for a microsecond before he pulled it out of her opening, wiping her warm, candy-tinged saliva on his uniform breast.

"What in the hell is wrong with you?" he asked, still feeling her on his finger while she relished him delightedly.

"Do you really want to know?" she asked, sexualizing her movements. How about I just ask you where your partner is and we can forget that I now know how you taste?" Giselle suggested, becoming more and more aggressive.

Rose looked at Giselle as if she was a cubist painting. She stood her ground with eyes that feasted on the chance that was being carted out before her.

"Cheddar is back at the stationhouse, fixing a voucher that he messed up," Rose disclosed hesitantly. "He'll be back out here with me later tonight."

Giselle smiled at this revelation, her dramatic eyes directing Rose's toward the sky.

"What?" he questioned, examining the sinking *cielo*. "There's something in the air tonight, right? Do you feel it as well?"

Giselle looked up at the darkening heavens. The sun had done an artful job of leaving soft traces of light in the upper atmosphere after it had retired for the night. This resulted in streaks of pink and orange amidst the converging purple.

"I don't know. It looks like rain to me. Heavy, heavy rain," Giselle stated, very much in code, concerning a sky absent even the most disguised storm cloud.

Rose played to her metaphor, suspicious of what awaited him. "Am I going to need an umbrella, or a raincoat or . . .?"

"Torrential downpour expected tonight. I'm talking dome stadium. You should really be careful. But I don't know anything, I gotta go now."

Rose held his hand out as if to supernaturally feel a drop of rain consistent with Giselle's incongruous, gloomy meteorological prognostication. His pensive eyes tracked the young fox as she scampered off to whatever stop she had to make in the path of her perilous travels. The night darkened in full and then, before long, it was coated in a claret fluid. Interrupting the symphony of scattered pigeon coos, wailing police sirens, disobeying pit bulls, and the clamorous sound of the indigenous language—not exactly spoken at church volume—was the unmistakable, oft-repeated chorus of many a Bronx nocturne: shots fired.

As Lieutenant Garret enjoyed Ludwig van Beethoven's Symphony no. 9 in D minor off his cell phone's playlist at the fifty-first precinct front desk, a two-man orchestra played a concert of death and decimation at a plagued address a mere two minutes afar by way of streaking police car. Drug kingpins, Diablo and Kilo—clad in black hooded sweatshirts and brandishing black Glock pistols—kicked in their rivals' door before unleashing a savage semiautomatic assault. It did not matter that the first victim, a black male, begged for his life against the island counter in the kitchen used to cook the drugs. The man received a bullet to his throat and another through his clenched gold teeth to effectively end his time on earth. As a second black male protested the onslaught, a bullet ripped through his eye socket before another exploded into his forehead, concurrently terminating his night and his life. A third black male raised his arms in surrender and cried for his life before turning his head to the side. This as a bullet spiraled through his ear canal, painting the refrigerator in a thick wine-red blood, coupled with a pink and brown brain sauce, which oozed down the refrigerator before the victim's collapsing body mopped the lower panel with that same substance. Kilo reached for a stack of blood-drenched cash on the counter.

"Just the fucking burners!" Diablo reprimanded as they ransacked every drawer in the apartment, removing a small cache of firearms which they re-appropriated for their personal arsenal.

The two felons stuffed the stolen firearms into their waistbands and pockets, fleeing into the corridor while leaving a trail of crimson in their wrathful wake. The first witness to unwisely open her door at the commotion was a frail, elderly Hispanic lady with large sky blue rollers in her bottle-dyed hair. Perhaps she believed the ash cross on her forehead would protect her, and so she dialed 911 from her cordless phone while keeping her bespectacled eyes on the assailants. At that moment, the rows of rollers in her hair were barbarously parted by a bullet which burrowed into her cranium, saturating her hair in its new color as rollers fell to the dirty, chess board style, tiled floor. This ruthless act was not enough for Diablo as he discharged one last round into her spine ensuring that the description given to the 911 dispatcher would be the last syllables she ever uttered. The perpetrators, devoid of any remorse, sprinted down the remaining length of the corridor and slammed the doorway to "staircase A" behind them, cracking the wire-mesh-reinforced glass in the process.

Officers Fernandez and Smith, engaged in a lusty mid-winter night's love entanglement, hurriedly put on their clothes and ran down "staircase B" with their fingers on the triggers of their firearms, ready to engage the callous murderers along the escape route to their hiding place. They crossed each other at precisely the twenty-third floor, on opposite ends of the doomed high-crime hell hole. Diablo and Kilo catapulted through the roof landing's door and climbed a long, bending staircase that led up into the elevator room. They slammed the door shut and hid there just after Rose and Cheddar had cannonballed themselves through the lobby doors of the nearby 711 Fairplace. Rose dropped his flashlight as he and Cheddar responded to the scene of what was already a quadruple homicide. Inside the apartment of three-fourths of the massacre, Fernandez and Smith had finally crashed through the door and Smith had greeted the crime scene by introducing her lunch to it in the form of clumpy oatmeal-colored vomit. Seconds earlier the perpetrators of violence had colored the drug kitchen in an unforgettable maroon. They used gushing strokes, spritzes, full out flooding, and a mopping effect to paint the crime scene as an abstract expressionist bloodbath with surrealist elements. As the whirly blades of a fan spun slowly, depositing drops of blood centrifugally in yet another pattern for the crime scene unit to investigate, a cinder block tumbled from out of the night sky, crunching down cantankerously on the roof of a responding police vehicle. The turret lights sandwiched into the partition which ended up in the back seat as the doors pushed out like the wings of a bird that was stepped on.

Beethoven's Ninth continued to play at the precinct desk from Lieutenant Garret's now abandoned cell phone. He too raced to the crime scene attempting to contribute his own notes to a cacophonic concert that included flashlights *clinking* to the ground, *retching* as vomit projected from rose-colored lips, and shots *howling* vociferously against the holy night as police cars imploded, heads exploded, and the music of the night transitioned shriekingly into a death ballad. The piece faded out to the sound of police batons cracking on the limbs of rioters, apparently motivated to spend the night in the bed bugged cells of Bronx Central Booking. The flutes, horns, and trombones of Beethoven came to an end with virtually no audience, save for sleepy arrestees in the crowded holding pen, in the now vacant fifty-first precinct lobby.

At a nearby church, a Catholic priest slid his tired thumb across the forehead of the last of the faithful—a straggler of sorts—receiving his ashes on this the first day of the holiest season of the year, on one of the most violent nights in what was fast becoming the most violent borough. Brooklyn had the reputation, but the Bronx had the bodies piling up like the product side of a meat slicer.

Rose stood at the crime scene, in the middle of maelstrom, with tumult swirling around him and he took a moment to close his eyes. His radio blared with confusing transmissions—everybody talking at once—and Rose thought of his father arriving at this horrific scene and trying to make sense of it. Rose turned his radio off; it would be the only serene seconds of that entire night for him. He let the quiet envelop him and walked over to the old lady who was a very unfortunate casualty of "wrong place, wrong time." She died in a small pool of her life fluid—the ironic part being that the euphemism only applies when the blood is inside your body—and Rose put a tissue over each of the two shell casings ejected next to her. He ripped out a page from his memorandum pad, a move which he was later reprimanded for, and wrote "victim number four" on it, placing it next to the deceased elderly. Rose brought his hand to his forehead to make the sign of the cross as a few coffee-like granules of ashes rubbed off on his middle finger. He took a knee and closed his eyes and recited a prayer over the old woman's fallen, holey body. Officer Brandon Rose was now deeply entrenched and looking to dig an even deeper trench, understanding that the battle for the streets would be a protracted one. He was committed and poised and began mentally *tacking up* to identify the killers, avenge this sadistic murder, and reap the glorious rewards.

The night would go on forever and Rose would end up tossing and turning on the damp, sweat-soaked couch in the fifty-first precinct lounge from the early afternoon, when he was done with his vouchers, until about 5 p.m. He rocked back and forth on it until Cheddar grabbed both of his shoulders and shook him like a human rattle. Rose awoke to the harsh reality, only to realize that this wasn't one of his dreams. His gun belt, pants, and other items from his uniform were strewn about the lounge floor. The ash on his forehead was almost entirely erased by perspiration and he could now confirm that he had in fact been present at the vile Ash Wednesday quadruple homicides.

"Get the hell up, man. You actually slept in this dump?" Cheddar castigated, readying his disdain for the ensuing answer.

"Yeah, I was up all morning doing the vouchers," Rose explained, eyeing the empty flashlight loop on his gun belt and the inside-outed patrol pants on the worn area rug.

"I *told* you: break the fuck out before the captain makes you process the whole goddamn crime scene, but you wanted to play detective and start putting stupid notes on the ground: "victim number four." No shit, Einstein, you think these detectives can't count? I know you got in trouble for ripping a page out of your memo book. Anyway, roll call is in twenty minutes, you better be there. I don't feel like working with one of these other losers tonight."

"Oh, but you like *this* loser, huh?" Rose teased, before acclimating himself. He slowly dragged himself off the couch and reflected inwardly regarding the sequence of events from the previous night. Cheddar shook his head at Rose moving mechanically around the room: picking up one boot, then the other, then a belt keeper, then his pants.

"Hurry the fuck up!" Cheddar yelled, lifting Rose off the ground and propelling him into a faster version of the very same tasks he was performing.

"Giselle was there!" Rose exclaimed, instantaneous to arriving at his epiphany.

"Giselle was there?" Cheddar repeated. "Who gives a flying fuck?"

"She told me it was going to rain," Rose celebrated, once again letting hopefulness lead him.

"Listen fool, it didn't rain last night. There was a goddamn *typhoon*."

"I know," Rose interjected. "And Giselle predicted that when I saw her earlier in the day. She was there when we booked it out of 711 Fairplace. She must know something. I saved her little ass once and she still owes me for that. I'm speaking to her tonight."

Cheddar exited the room, not exactly exalted by Rose's findings. Rose quickly dressed with a new sense of purpose, eager to take the first step in the journey that would lead him from his still embryonic police dreams to the envisioned reality of wearing the highly sought-after gold detective's shield.

"Giselle," he smiled. It gave him all the purpose he needed to continue.

Giselle was already pin balling around the neighborhood at this time, juking through police periphery with her familiar school bag in tow. She halted to observe the blue and white crime scene van finally vacate the scene of the murders. Yellow and black crime scene tape still enclosed the perimeter—wrapped around outlining lampposts—but would soon litter the ground and be relegated to kids' jump ropes for the night. Giselle pulled out her rhinestone encrusted cell phone and made a business phone call:

"Diablo? Give it about fifteen more minutes, there's still some *DT's* snooping around. Yeah, CSU, crime scene unit or whatever they're called, already left and there's only one blue and white here but they look like they're about to go on a donut break. They left one fat-ass upstairs to guard the apartment but he's just playing on his phone. Yeah, the rookies start soon and I'm sure they'll be all over this place like a swarm of flies on a warm turd. So hurry up if you can."

Giselle concluded her phone call with the crime boss just as Sergeant Valdez was fervidly bleeding out her roll call speech to her group of static bowling pins in uniform.

"Last night we had a quadruple homicide. Three mutts and one poor old lady met their demise at the hands of a couple of savages. The perps? I don't know, apparently they're fucking magicians and vanished into the air. Seven thousand bags of heroin: *untouched*. One hundred and sixty-three *thousand* dollars were freaking left on the table. I know because I was here counting the money with Officer Rose until about noon. And the perps? Mosquitos in the wind. They probably took a shit on us and we didn't even feel it."

As a mystified Valdez attempted to convey the gravity of last night's happenings to her flock, Diablo and Kilo were emerging from the elevator room, sullied and slowly, like the characters in Samuel Beckett's *Endgame* emerging from trashcans in the wake of apocalyptic disaster. The difference was Diablo and Kilo ushered in the disaster and they wore the stench and guilt of the atrocity like a proud badge shaped from shit. As the fugitives dusted off the crud, the fifty-first precinct muster room swelled with tension as Valdez continued her diatribe amidst a cloud of cigarette smoke and a verbal form of sulfuric acid.

"The defectives upstairs, who can't seem to solve shit by the way, said eight guns were missing from the apartment. How do they know that? Apparently a confidential informant told them. Eight shell casings were found, which means these animals were *efficient*. They took out four people with exactly eight shots. We need to shoot someone forty-one times to hit them in the pinky. There were two sets of Timberland construction boot prints in the pools of blood, not to mention Officer Smith's lunch. Did they teach you to barf on crime scenes at the academy or is that something you picked up on your own? Or maybe Fernandez taught you that since you two are so cozy. Let me know."

Smith hung her head as Valdez stared down each and every rookie standing at attention and clenching their sphincter muscles, meeting her tough façade with subtle submissiveness.

"Let me wrap this up. They shot an eighty-five-year-old woman. Every victim was shot in the head. They now have at least ten guns in their possession and I don't think they like cops. On top of all that, it's the Lenten season. Maybe Jesus can save us, maybe that fucker can't," Valdez speculated, exhaling a mass of smoke into the air that carried the residue from the preceding vitriol.

Rose re-stepped into the very same spot in which he was already standing, nodded his head affirmatively and tugged his eight-point hat down on his forehead. He was digging in, as if he had just heard the opening salvo in a war in which he would be a much relied upon soldier. Valdez put hammer to nail as the rookies began to rock in place just a bit from the weight of their gun belts:

"This ain't Sesame Street even if your lieutenant does look like Big Bird—yellow motherfucker. Those perps are gonna try and use those guns on us. They want to kill cops! You find those guys and those guns, you're saving cops' lives. If one of you arrests those perps I can guarantee you I'll personally sign your recommendation for the detective program. Lose this monkey suit, get a gold shield. Now who here wouldn't want to get accepted into the eighteen-month program? The shield is all but guaranteed."

Rose looked over to Cheddar and showed him all his teeth, excitement changing the tone of his skin. He beamed and made a gun signal with his hand, pretending to fire a shot. Cheddar feigned catching the bullet with his teeth and spitting it out on the floor.

"Are you two clowns done?" scolded a still hostile Valdez, distributing wanted posters for robberies, missing persons photos, and intel collected by field intelligence officers.

In the rear of 711 Fairplace, Giselle met up with Diablo and Kilo to collect the stolen firearms. She placed the weapons in her *Hanna Montana* backpack while deliberately avoiding eye contact with the intimidating duo.

"How was the response time?" asked Diablo, hiding his permanently scowled face under a hood.

"Lightning fast. Shots fired and two minutes later these two rookies were at the scene like a couple of track stars with roman candles up their asses. One of them dropped his flashlight so . . ."

"Fuck the flashlight," Diablo dismissed, "What about the pigs in patrol cars?"

"About a minute or two later, but still quick. They dropped the dragnet. There's no way you guys would have made it out of the building," Giselle opined, feeling the weight of the steel pieces dragging her school bag down.

"We took a big fucking chance hiding out in the elevator shaft, D," remarked a fatigued Kilo. "Those motherfuckers could have used the dogs like last time."

"They couldn't use the dogs because they didn't have a scent to compare it to," Diablo stated, mistakenly. "Plus, I threw bleach all over the stairs. All they had was their desire to catch us, which we know isn't much. Cops are scared, and they're lazy. The elevator room is an extra set of stairs for them to climb and you know they're allergic to exercise."

Diablo congratulated himself with a laugh and then revealed his end game strategy.

"If any cop would have cracked that door, they would have been giving head to my heater."

At this exact moment, the door to the fifty-first precinct muster room creaked loudly and Lieutenant Garret peeked in, unconcealedly annoyed. After cross-referencing what he was feeling with the sterile white clock slumping on the wall, he vociferously chimed in.

"Alright, enough with the motivational speeches. Take your post numbers and fall out. The job is out on the streets, not in this room!" he yelled, almost as a maxim. "Fall out guys! And when you get to post, don't bury your heads in your phones. We got some serious airmail last night. Make sure you position yourself under an overhang, know where your nearest cover is, and always look up. Let's go! We're police officers we don't hide from the bad guys, they hide from us."

Lieutenant Garret would always mix concern and criticism like a drink, and although he was stern, he was fatherly in the most understated way. He patted Rose and Cheddar on the back on their way past him. And the partners trudged to post, still not completely accustomed to the sinking weight of their gun belt digging in to their hips and their restrictive ballistic vests squeezing them. Rose and Cheddar jotted an entry in their memo books as Giselle came hopping toward them, snapping large pink strawberry scented bubbles from her spicy mouth. She twirled a large black flashlight like a marching band baton and shined it directly on Rose's face.

"Well, if it isn't *Lolita* herself," Rose greeted, not quite as enamored by the ghetto debutante as he had been in the past.

"A very overrated novel in my opinion. I hate Nabokov. I'm more of an F. Scott Fitz—"

"You're playing me," Rose accused. "You knew exactly what was going to happen last night and you gave me some bullshit cryptic clue about a dome stadium and goddamn precipitation. We could have been killed! And I know you're still working for those low lives."

"Actually I'm on the market: free agent. You wanna sign me, sugar?"

"Sign you?" an incensed Cheddar sliced in. "He's about to lock you up. You try and run that little miss sunshine bullshit on us, but we both know you're dirtier than that tampon in between your hairy legs."

This delighted Giselle as she could now unleash her own vibrant venom on Rose's surrogate.

"Where's *your* tampon, *sonny boy*?" she asked with a suddenly southern accent. "In your mouth? Or is it a midget tap dancing on shit on your tongue that's producing that awful stench?"

"No, I think it's your mother having another one of you behind this dumpster," shot back a fired up Cheddar, wearing a competitive smile that curled into something more sinister.

Giselle recovered from the blow as Cheddar dug in. "Which one are you again, George Washington? Or are you President Fuller?"

"There was no President Fuller, *jabroni*," she corrected, with neck-snapping pizzazz.

"Exactly what I'd expect President *Fulla'shit* to say. Now I know you think all cops are stupid, but I can guarantee that before the Easter bunny leaves you a log in your little hay basket, we're dragging your friends off to jail and introducing you to the juvenile detention system. You little jail bait trick."

"Cheddar, relax!" exclaimed Rose. "She's just a kid," he reminded, turning his body in her direction. "Listen to me, Giselle Elizabeth Ignacio. You want to be a big girl and look out for drug dealing scum? Well, your friends—Thomas Jefferson, Abe Lincoln—they're not going on some drug dealer's version of Mount Rushmore. They're going to Riker's Island and then up north after that. They serve up something stiff there and the peanut butter and jelly goes hand in hand with K-Y Jelly. You get me? Do your friends like that? I know *you* don't want any part of that."

Giselle looked at Rose through the squinted overhang of her freshly-threaded eyebrows. She appeared meek, belying the ferocious animal caged within her. Rose's sympathy for her grew in that moment and he sought to use a gentler approach to soften up his potential helper.

"Give me a sec', Cheddar. Let me talk to her alone please," Rose pleaded, leading Giselle off to where he could communicate with her in softer keys. Rose stepped outside of the circumference of Cheddar's listening capabilities and tilted Giselle's head upward by the chin, giving birth to a radiant smile.

"Look into my eyes. You told me you wanted out and I trusted you. I truly believed that you were done with those thugs. You are going to get arrested. Or hurt. And I'm talking badly. Now please Giselle: big quadruple homicide last night. Innocent old lady gunned down on her own welcome mat. The Ash Wednesday massacre is what we're calling it. Were your boys involved? Was it the founding fathers?"

Giselle's eyes sleepily glazed over but with the sweetness of cake frosting. She slowly, unsubtly licked her Cupid's bow and leaned in invitingly as a tiny pool of saliva formed inside the space between her lower lip and her gums. Rose physically declined, the fruity smell of Giselle's chewing gum penetrating his face from right above his lip. A staring contest ensued and one could reasonably perceive that lust danced in Giselle's irises. She stood before him like a rare winter flower, perhaps an out of season Iris, fighting the intrinsic urge to unfurl completely before Rose, who was unknowingly watering her with his dewy attentiveness.

"Tell me," Rose commanded.

"And what do I get in exchange for being a Benedict Arnold?"

"You can finally declare your independence from your oppressors. And I myself will pledge my allegiance to you," Rose replied, riding the wordplay into the ground, but with a sincerity that could almost forgive the corniness of the exchange.

"Maybe it was Hondurians," Giselle offered.

"Hondurians? You mean *Hondurans*? People from Honduras?"

"Whatever . . . maybe . . . possibly . . ."

"I need more than that."

"I need more from *you*," she turned. "The last time was a freebie. Maybe getting hit by that car gave me diarrhea of the mouth. But I'm requesting payment now," she declared, firmly stomping her foot in the gum-blemished concrete square in which she stood.

"And what, may I ask, is the currency?" Rose begged, tiptoeing around the rabbit hole that was slowly exposing itself and threatening to vacuum him in.

"I want your time. But I'm talking quality time, not tagging along on your foot post with your wannabe boyfriend and his halitosis."

"That's just not possible."

"Then the information isn't possible. Case closed. Thanks for coming. Drive home safely. Here."

Giselle passed Rose his flashlight, somehow eroticizing the handoff. She manipulated him with a look of craving that was so brief and gentle it could have been repurposed by the wind.

"Thank you. If I'm on post without this and *Inspections* come around I get a CD."

"Command discipline?" Giselle translated.

"How do you know so much of our jargon, huh?" Rose asked suspiciously.

"I watch a lot of cop shows."

"In between selling drugs?"

"I do not sell. Never have, never will. I'm just the eyes."

"Well then look, 'eyes'. I'm going to figure this thing out. With you or without you."

"Determination. I like that," Giselle facetiously remarked. "I like that and I like you. And since you *did* save me from going to A.C.S. I'll throw you a bone."

"It better have meat on it," Rose returned, not realizing that she was about to add spices too.

"I told you about the founding fathers and as you can imagine, they're all about the Benjamins. But the break in this case, for you, lies with Bush."

"Bush, like *President* Bush?" decrypted Rose, stepping into a well set trap.

"No, like *my* Bush," Giselle vulgarly quipped, chewing up the scenery and spitting it out, clearly discarding tact by just about anybody's standards.

Rose stood there, exercising no authority, in the wake of her potent inappropriateness. He was rescued by Cheddar, having grown impatient with pacing on the sidelines.

"Looks like Hutch missed Starsky. Exit stage left for the little one," she theatricalized, performing a pirouette, a curtsey and blowing Rose a moist goodbye kiss. Rose batted away the imaginary smooch as Giselle skipped off, her feet barely touching the ground.

"Tell me what the hell's been going on between you two," demanded Cheddar.

"Nothing—just talking. It's called *community policing*. She's going to be a good informant. You'll see. Watch," defended Rose.

"So you're serious? She's really your C.I.? You're not just trying to get some ass?"

"Ass? What on earth is wrong with you? I'm not trying to get no damn jail bait buns."

"Bullshit! You like her," contested Cheddar. "I'm going to collar you. You're going to be on that show 'To Catch a Predator' with that guy, the white guy."

"Chris Hansen?" Rose answered.

"You see? You know who I'm talking about, you fucking pervert!" celebrated Cheddar, nakedly amused by his deduction.

"Keep laughing at your own jokes. She gave me some damn good intel. I'm going to continue using her. I'm going to follow the crumbs."

"You might as well follow the yellow brick road if you believe the fantasy that little wicked witch—or wicked bitch—just sold you."

"Whatever you say. Look, this isn't Kansas. This is Zoo York City. The stakes are high and I'm going to help her help me. I just have to figure out what she meant by George Bush."

"George Bush my left nut. Don't forget what happened to Bill Clinton," Cheddar warned before crudely acting out oral sex and the motion of a penis ejaculating.

Rose plotted there, in front of his partner, backlit by the moon, undeterred by Cheddar's cynicism and chastising. He had only begun prosecuting his case but the young striver could already visualize victory. He mapped out in his mind the entirety of the long game he was playing— from the moment he learns the identity of the killers to the moment a detective shield is pinned on his blouse by the Police Commissioner. He fantasized, until a Cheddar elbow to the ribcage reminded him that his boots were firmly planted in the South Bronx and that he still had hours of patrolling remaining on his itinerary. But Rose was hopeful, and he conducted his ensuing vertical patrols with a spring in his step, confident that what he was calculating would result in the realization of his police dreams. His smile shone brighter than the very light reflecting off his underappreciated tin shield, and still that paled mightily in comparison to a natural light that was starting to emit more perceivably from within Rose. He was gaining traction now, due mostly to the fact that he had settled comfortably into his job as a police officer and he believed he was setting up a ground game—by securing a snitch—that was the key to opening up all of the streets' secrets to him. Rose possessed this incredible self-belief: a self-efficacy on permanent steroids and it drove him. Cheddar, however, had yet to notice that special sparkle that his partner would become known for. But it was there, like a wick that no one knew was lit but suddenly made the table setting that much warmer.

Chapter IV

At her lair, the provocateur-like Giselle reentered the household dynamic where she was dominated into manifest submissiveness to the predatory Greer and Puff.

"Giselle, any boys in blue for me to toast with my piece?" inquired Greer, brandishing a firearm carelessly, as if it wasn't actually capable of blowing somebody away.

"Nah, J.G., I just got rid of two little *rooks*. They tried to question me but I played head games with them."

"Or did you give them head?" reversed Puff, enraging Giselle and soaking it in with a gold teeth revealing grin.

"You always gotta come out your mouth with some disrespectful shit!" Giselle snapped.

"I gotta come out my mouth, huh?" repeated Puff. "Well, how about I come in *your* mouth?" Giselle shot him dead with her fiery brown eyes and mouthed a barely audible "fuck you" in his direction.

"Go, hoe," he berated, "go outside and look out for the boys. We're selling from inside today since you can't do your job properly. Hard knock to enter, just point the customers to the door."

On that very rooftop, urine was sprinkling off miniature rum bottles as Rose and Cheddar christened the unholy edifice while powwowing about their next maneuver.

"What are we doing, man? We're really waiting for her signal?" Cheddar asked skeptically.

"She whispered it to me. I trust her, for some reason," Rose revealed, taking the moment to scan the rooftop. "Hey, have you noticed there's no elevator room in this building?" asked Rose.

"I don't know, could it be because there's no elevator maybe? *Ding ding ding!*"

"Right. But 1805 Harmony Avenue does have one. It has thirty-nine floors, how could it not, right?"

"You're gonna get that gold shield after all," Rose's non-believing comrade encouraged.

"Keep following: the roof would be the fortieth floor. And then you have the elevator room, up that short flight of steps, leading right into the elevator shaft. That's the forty-first floor."

"Now that I know you can count—"

"George Bush my man. George Herbert Walker Bush was the forty-first president. That's where the perps hid!"

"In George Bush's ass?" dismissed Cheddar.

"No, in the elevator room! The killers hid there until the crime scene was processed. They couldn't leave the building so they stayed *in* the building," postulated Rose, his mind already so far into the future and being pulled by his rabid excitement. Cheddar's response was the equivalent of a saliva-beaded yawn. He had yet to board Rose's runaway locomotive, its cylinders and valves, rods and wheels just barely beginning to squeal out the initial sounds of progressive motion.

In the vestibule, Giselle directed a junkie, bobbing like a buoy on salt water, to the apartment door in front of where Greer and Puff pedaled their packaged poison. As the addict turned toward the door, Giselle whistled loudly, summoning Rose and Cheddar who hotfooted down the stairs, clocking their hooves against dingy imitation ceramic. In a blur, the two metamorphosed quarter horses had the weaver against the wall, frisking his waistband for gravity knives or any other contraband weapons.

"We got you, my man. Do you have a reason for being in this building? Can't you read the signs? This is a 'clean halls' building," explained Rose, feeling around his gun belt for his handcuff case. "The mayor would be very upset if he knew you were trespassing here, my friend."

"No, no, Captain. I'm just visiting a buddy," he explained—leaning, like so many Bronx street signs. "Aw shit, thanks for the promotion. But before I release you, just direct me to the apartment where your friend resides."

The male pointed right to the lion's den occupied by Greer and Puff as Giselle stood captive to the suspense, wondering how this situation would disentangle.

"That's the one. The one with the magic fairies," he volunteered, to loud, girlish laughter from an amused Giselle.

"I'm all for magic fairies," admitted Cheddar, "especially if they give it up easy. But if we knock on that door and Tinker Bell doesn't sprinkle pixie dust on my dick, you're gonna be wearing these magic bracelets and your arrest number is going on my overtime slip."

The junkie wobbled in place some more as Rose approached the door. Giselle appeared as though she was holding in a fast approaching bowel movement. Rose banged forcefully on the door with the butt of his police radio.

"What do you want, bitch?" asked a startled Puff, now nose to nose with Rose, whose upper lip angled at the corners into a zealous smile.

"That's *Officer* Bitch to you, sir," corrected Rose, relishing the slip-up and readying to unleash a little bit of wrath and fury if given the opportunity.

"Officer, I'm so sorry. I was alarmed by the loud banging. I thought it was one of the delinquent kids that live in the building. I was just studying for my history exam that's coming up—"

"Everybody's a historian in this goddamn building, huh?" interrupted Rose, now locked into a stare with his freshly revealed rival. They held poker faces free of any flinching or submitting.

"Is this gentleman a friend of yours?" investigated Rose, attempting to corroborate a known lie.

As he did this, Puff stole a look at Giselle—a virtual death glance—before proclaiming nonchalantly:

"He looks like a no good drug addict to me. You should lock him up and throw away the key."

"Oh, you rhyme too. Looks like I'll do just that, 'cuff him, Ched'," ordered Rose as Cheddar pulled out a shiny set of handcuffs, never before worn by anyone.

"*Somebody's going to jail,*" Cheddar sung, as the man now flailed his arms, complicating the task.

"You come any closer and I'll be all over your ass like a red goat," warned the druggie.

"Did he just say 'red goat'?" verified Giselle.

"Yeah, a half unicorn," explained the man, clearly residing in a different hallucinatory reality as a result of self-administered chemicals. "No! No, *mutha'fucka's*. You're just tryna' make your quotas! Go get the goat rapists! Go get the butt burglars. Stop tryna' make me one of your quotas, you racist pigs!"

Rose moved in, bending the man's arm sharply and placing it behind his back for him. Cheddar fumbled the handcuffs in the struggle and Giselle immediately unsnapped Rose's handcuff case and calmly clicked the metal restraints on to the resisting man's track mark-adorned wrists.

"Oh shit," Rose exhaled, his eyes following Giselle weave in between him and Cheddar and the detainee like an engaged hornet through trees. "Cheddar, how does this methadonian mutant even know about our quotas?"

"Everyone knows about your quotas," Giselle boasted, as she, the two officers and the zombie-like arrestee formed a strange quartet in the lobby of that doomed pile of bricks.

"Did she really just cuff our perp?" questioned Cheddar. "What is she, your new partner? Is she your k-9 or something?"

"You're the one with dog breath. Call the patrol supervisor to verify this arrest and tell him to bring a toothbrush for 'Scooby'," Giselle joked, clearly enjoying her time with the officers as the impromptu "ride along" was coming to an abrupt end for her.

Once Rose, Cheddar, and their prisoner exited the building, Giselle came crashing back to her own reality at the unforgiving hands of Puff and his alcoholic acolyte, Greer.

"You fucking cunt! You actually had a cop knock on our door when you *know* we have drugs and guns all over the goddamn place! Are you *trying* to get us locked up? Tell me why I shouldn't blast you right now?" asked Puff, raising the barrel of his gun up to Giselle's forehead.

"Because then you can't fuck me. If you kill me you can't fuck me anymore, right?" Giselle asked as rhetorically as humanly possible.

"Fuck you? You keep trying to fuck us. You've got the easiest job in the world and you can't even do it right!" Puff raged, his voice escalating to a yell now. "Why don't you just invite them in for coffee next time and Jeff here will wash their uniforms for them while they wait?"

Puff pulled the barrel of the gun away from Giselle's pretty crown. The young girl buried her head in her hands, her nails decorated with rainbow colored polish. She wept for a second before gathering rage and unleashing a small tempest on her tormentors.

"Fuck this! I'm tired of this crap! I don't want to do this shit anymore. Find a new bitch to look out for you two ungrateful assholes. I'm done!" Giselle declared, the invisible shackles on her ankles not instantly snapped by her independence-declaring proclamation.

"You're done when I say you're done. I don't trust new bitches and I don't let my employees leave just because they fuckin' feel like it," explained Puff.

"Let me leave! Let me leave!" screamed Giselle, her face reddening and her petite feet now stomping on the wooden floorboard, a childish signature of sorts for her. Puff grabbed a short stack of money from the larger stacks that Greer was counting and smacked Giselle across the face with it. He lifted Giselle virtually out of her sequins embossed shoes and slammed her on a tacky pastiche Persian rug with semen stains on it. He snapped the rubber band and coldly threw the cash at Giselle, the bills fluttering through the air like the VIP section of a strip club. Giselle crawled to escape while clutching her right side in pain.

"There you go, *hoe*. Crawl for cash. Pick that money up off the floor, you fucking slutbag!" Greer encouraged, before taking a long swig of a dark cognac and a puff of his dirty blunt to further transport him away from there. Giselle pushed the money away from her body as if performing a breast stroke; she swam in a waterless pool, drowning in embarrassment and shame.

"Go on. Buy some shoes or books or whatever the fuck you like," suggested Puff, viewing Giselle as no higher than a dog as he began gathering his illegally acquired currency. She collected herself, holding the pieces of a fractured self-worth in her hands like ridged bottle caps. She had some repairing to do and some re-pairing to do. Giselle staggered to her feet like a boxer just barely beating the ten count and walked—broken—to her room, having left her dignity on that stained rug but in her mind relinquishing her role as door mat to her two heavy-footed abusers.

When Rose entered his hollow apartment early that same morning, he had images of Giselle and Cecelia simultaneously helixing through his mind. He poured himself a glass of browning pinot noir, taking a swig of his favorite wine, its woody, cigar box-like flavor remaining on his tongue long after the swallow. He thought about his life as a calm snow globe that he was about to shake, except the flakes weren't harmless confetti disguised as snow but rather shards of glass from a broken, flaw-exposing expository mirror. He would often assess his life under a microscope's lens on these dimming, ebbing moments of the night while most slept. The creaking of his rickety wooden floorboard, the tapping of dripping water drops splashing against the bathroom sink's pop-up stopper, the buzzing of the refrigerator fan as it responded to temperature change, the venetian blinds clicking and clacking off the window mullions; all of these things provided a sort of comforting, drowsing rhythm as Rose sunk into his pillow top mattress, glass in hand, and contemplated. His apartment breathed in sync with him, a living organism with imitation Van Gogh's and Magritte's adorning the sterile white walls. They were perhaps his most comforting friends as he lay in bed and journeyed into himself, his own voice narrating the introverted voyage into his center.

Giselle paralleled this as she longingly lay in her bed, bleeding emotion onto her notebook pages, curled at the corners like so many school children.

There certainly wasn't any art adorning her room's walls, but the positioning of her body was reminiscent of the deteriorated, polio-suffering feminine subject of Wyeth's *Christina's World* and she was just as incapacitated at the moment. Her eyes were badly swollen not from tiredness but from tears, which washed away her makeup; her thoughts pouring out of her eyes like a cracked fish tank and making the thin blue lines of her composition notebook bleed their color. She yearned for a way out of her world.

In California, Cecelia's pensive, melancholy brown eyes glowed in her room like small lanterns. She curled her willowy carriage in her bed holding her pillow like a life raft and, in this moment, resembled Giselle or at least an older sister. Her textbooks, notebooks, and hi-lighters surrounded her on the mattress as drowsiness descended upon her like cough medicine. Cecelia's cell phone flashed silently as her eyes sealed for the night and the words "missed call: my hubby" appeared on the LCD screen.

And soon Rose slept and Giselle slept and Cecelia slept, the three of them completely unaware of the scalene triangle of affection, fondness, and tenderness which together they formed and would one day create the most difficult type of equation to be solved. But for tonight they were safe. The soothing arm of night cradled them in their slumber, protecting the trio from problems that rear their head, counterintuitively, with the new light of day. Rose would dream on this night, as he always dreamt: with gunfire and bloodshed and triumphant gold badges being honorably pinned on his uniform. He tossed like vegetables in a wok that night, the heat of his apartment's radiator cooking him in the juices of his own precarious dream. He baked in his bed, before being pushed out of REM sleep like a baby from a vagina. In the late morning, he lay in his bed, delivered. He was greasy, completely covered in the vernix that enveloped him in his dream and blood that stained him during the dark alley shootout. He opened his eyes and interpreted his world, the light hurting his eyes. He was remedial in his initial understanding until all of his senses awakened, and he unfurled like the rose that he was, stretching out against the world that he would soon decide he wanted to conquer. And then Rose, like his increasingly naked ambitions and the heightening stakes, was risen.

Interlude

In the muster room that afternoon, Rose's eyes imitated two synchronized passenger boats motoring through a sea of mug shot photos, robbery pattern pin maps, and other useful precinct literature which decorated the room to the point of wallpaper-like inundation. The fliers appeared to undulate as if wind had snuck in underneath them and they were traveling in rhythmic waves while Rose's eyes rode them like crest foam. Rose stood at attention and stood out with his noteworthy presence while the other rookies showcased their freshman fatigue and displayed scuffed boots, five o'clock shadows and food stained uniforms. Lieutenant Garret entered the room and carried it, addressing his slumping platoon.

"Attention to roll call. The color of the day is orange, the return date for c summonses is May twenty-sixth. You guys look like a bunch of hair bags. A couple of months and you don't give two shits about your appearance anymore? Take some goddamn pride in how you look. This uniform and this patch are world-renowned. If this was baseball we'd be the New York Yankees. Some of you apparently want to be the Mets," Garret joked, to a couple of semi-forced laughs, which camouflaged the flirting that was transpiring between Smith and Fernandez. "I just got my asshole shredded at COMPSTAT. We're getting killed with seven majors. We have absolutely zero UF250s. Is it really that hard to stop, question, and frisk someone in the Bronx? Toss these perps, they're carrying! How else are you gonna get guns off the streets? You know what, I can see that you guys all have your heads buried in your asses, to hell with this shit!"

The lieutenant flicked the roll call sheets at the officers, catching Rose right in his concentrating eyes. Garret stormed out of the room, taking all the air with him. The rookies look around insecurely, a few of them nervously clearing their throats before collective snickering evolved into all out laughter.

"You guys gotta be on your p's and q's when the lieutenant has his period," joked Officer Fernandez, emboldened by his status as senior officer in the room.

"He always has his period," offered Smith. "His wife doesn't give him any *nookie?*"

"Nookie?" piled on Cheddar. "I think what the l-t wants is a nice big dick and he wants it from my man *Detective* Rose. That's why he threw the roll call at him, to have an excuse to apologize to him later on . . . behind closed doors of course."

Cheddar's remarks were met with *ooh-ing* as Rose stood there like a redwood during a rain storm. He fixated on a precinct bulletin offering a reward for the Ash Wednesday killers, as they were known. As laughter engulfed him, Rose maintained his aneurism-like seriousness. This was until Sergeant Valdez stormed into the room like a debris-fed tornado.

"I don't find anything funny! The lieutenant just chewed my ass out. Read your posts and fall the fuck out. I'm gonna need Preparation H *with* aloe after the ass-thrashing you guys just caused me."

"Sarge, I heard A and D ointment works better on your ass ridges and it's cheaper too," Cheddar volunteered to sheer wrath on the part of his impact sergeant.

"Oh yeah? You're gonna have diaper rash on your lips if you don't get out of my face, you two-bit clown," warned the fire-breathing sergeant as the rookies scrambled away like pigeons from a stomping toddler.

As they hurriedly exited the precinct, Detective White poured a bucket of water out of the window, drowning Rose in every single drop contained therein. Rose bailed it with his eight-point hat, spat water from his cheeks and examined the picture of him and Cecelia that was now damp and fading.

"Is that why you want to make detective so badly, Rose? So you can dump water on rookies and beat your meat all day long?" Cheddar questioned, in essence rubbing salt into the wounds.

"I guess that's why they call them defectives. They really do have something wrong with them," Rose concluded before yelling the word 'defectives' from deep down in his abdomen.

Once calmed, Rose made his way to patrol post number six and moseyed past a Catholic church with a huge wooden crucifix on it. As he made the sign of the cross, Giselle interrupted him somewhere around the Holy Spirit.

"Boo!"

"Well, look who it is, Richard freaking Nixon," Rose identified.

"I am not a crook," returned Giselle, her eyes wide open with elation at the sight of her cop crush.

"I'll try again. Are you Alexander Graham Bell?"

"Not at all. But you're going to call me on the device he invented the night before we go on our first date," she smartly countered.

"First date?" Rose repeated. "Someone's getting high on their own supply. I'll give you credit though, that was cute."

"Oh, so you think I'm cute?" Giselle probed, modeling for him before performing a tantalizing little number that included moistening the tip of her finger with her tongue and then twirling it.

"Not at all," Rose batted. "I think you're obnoxious. You're young. And you're dumb for doing what you do."

"So let me get this straight," Giselle began. "I'm obnoxious, young, dumb and full of—"

"Don't say it!" Rose warned, hopscotching in.

"Gum!" Giselle punch-lined, accompanied by a girlish cackle which relieved Rose, actively defending against her undisguised sexuality. She popped a large pink bubble so loud it could have been a gunshot. She winked at him, swatted away by a disapproving shake of the head. She persisted, chewing noisily as Rose sought the repellant to thwart the stinging gnat.

"Listen to me: I'm done with this lifestyle. I'm done with these assholes. I'm done with everything. I want to help you get collars, *good* collars."

"I don't need your little bullshit trespass collars; I can get those on my own."

"I can get you something better."

"No. You already lied to me once. I'm not buying it," Rose refused angrily.

"You'll get promoted faster than any bastard at your precinct if you just follow what I'm saying," Giselle assured, dangling the carrot presciently. "And all you have to do is take me on a date."

"A date to where, huh? The Bronx Zoo? What, you wanna feed the llamas? Ride an elephant?" Rose asked, setting up a fastball for Giselle.

"Not unless you're an elephant," she seduced, as Rose caught his jaw off his shoestrings after initially reeling back from Giselle's wanton audacity. She tilted her head sideways while implicitly eyeballing Rose's crotch, which might as well have introverted from discomfort at the situation. Rose was not prepared to defend against her at this volume; he was ill-matched for Giselle's overt sexual firepower at a moment when his guard was down from the long week's exhaustion.

"I can't do it. I won't do it," Rose asserted. "Taking you on a date is career suicide."

"Actually, it's career resurrection," she countered. "I'll tell you exactly how you can lock these scumbags up, but I can't put the 'cuffs on them, you gotta do that yourself," Giselle teased, reminding Rose of her previous intervention. "All you have to do is take me to see the city from the top of the Empire State Building."

"The Empire State Building on Thirty-fourth Street?" Rose asked, immediately feeling silly.

"No, not that one at all. The one on top of that one. The black one," Giselle joked as Rose's wit and intellect slowly began returning to him after some mental space traveling.

"I've lived in New York for sixteen years and I'd like to go up there before Bush knocks that building down too," Giselle reported with just a pinch of sweetness sprinkled in amidst conspiratorial distrust.

"A little young to be doubting the US government, no?"

"Forget those white old geezers—well except for one," Giselle slipped in.

"I haven't forgotten about that one," Rose assured her. "You're badmouthing the son, but it's the father who I'm more interested in."

"What are you talking about?" Giselle asked disguisedly.

"1805 Harmony Avenue has thirty-nine floors, correct?"

"I don't know. Ask the architect," she deadpanned.

"I already did. And the rooftop makes forty," Rose calculated. "And there's an extra landing on the roof that leads up into the elevator room. That would, technically, be the forty-first floor. *Forty-one*— like George Herbert Walker Bush. He was your clue the other night and there's your 'white old geezer'," Rose surmised.

"That's not it. You didn't get it," Giselle ruled.

"No, bullshit I figured it out. I'm going up there."

"You could try. But you should be careful. You may not be ready for what's up there."

"I'm ready for anything. *Anything*!" Rose repeated self-assuredly.

"Confidence. I like that. And determination too. *Se-xy*!" Giselle complimented. "So if your hunch is correct and you go up there and you actually find some evidence, then I'll meet you Wednesday morning at eight o'clock right in front of the most beautiful building in New . . . York . . . Ci-*tay*."

"Even if I find something useful: a bloody shirt, a loaded gun, can I really meet you in midtown Manhattan? I mean, I'm a cop. You're. . .

whatever you are. Not to mention it's more than twenty bucks per person to get up there. Are you paying? You probably make more money than I do."

"Oh honey, don't be a silly goose. Just tin your way in. You got a shield, use it."

""Tin my way in"?" Rose echoed. "How do you even know that expression? I don't believe it's just from cop shows. You're a kid. Shouldn't you be watching *Hanna Montana* or something?"

"With all due respect, Officer Rose, Hanna Montana can suck it. Just not as good as me," Giselle bragged as Rose tensed there, disavowing any and all hints of amusement at Giselle's antics. She smiled flirtatiously before Rose corrected her face with a stern glare.

"Stop that. Knock it off already," he ordered authoritatively.

"What are you talking about?"

"*That*—that thing you do. You are a really smart, really beautiful girl. You're even charming at times, in a really endearing way honestly. You don't need to say vulgar things to make yourself more appealing. First of all, you're too young for that. Secondly, you can't throw yourself at someone and expect to be respected. Be a lady goddammit. Value yourself, Giselle," Rose scolded, as his one-person audience stood there—mouth agape—utterly infatuated still but recalibrating to the message now.

Giselle uncharacteristically struggled with what Rose had just said as if hindered by a language barrier. She tried to separate the compliment from the criticism like separating a pistachio from its shell. Rose inched closer to her, looking deeply into her sad, moistening eyes; the breath coming from her mouth audible to him but noiseless compared to the drum of her excited heartbeat. In that moment she wished for him and he wished he possessed a map so he could take a road trip through her deep-rooted pain and understand her better. She just looked up at him, meekly, vulnerably. She broke the eye contact but he quickly pulled her back into his exploratory eye lock.

"Is that a black eye I see?" Rose questioned, examining Giselle the way one inspects a rental car before driving it out of the lot. He looked closer to see what other damage he might find, Giselle's chin planted in the palm of his hand, his cupped fingers framing her like a portrait.

"That's just my mascara running. It's not a black eye," Giselle misinformed.

Rose pulled down on his sleeve and used it to gently rub out Giselle's eye makeup, revealing a bruise around her eyes, which were cocoa brown today. He held her face tenderly, and followed every line on it with his eyes. She stared at him, as captive as any prisoner could ever be. She couldn't move if she wanted to at that point. Rose's face angered but he also took an almost unnoticeable plunge. He had just become invested in Giselle in a way that was dangerous to him. This opened up a world of questions, which he knew better than to begin asking at this stage. But she was a problem, standing before him.

"Tell me on Wednesday. This isn't going to continue. No phone call. I'll see you there at eight o'clock. Don't be late, otherwise I'm going home," Rose warned.

Giselle was, for the very first time since we met her, utterly speechless. She was a butterfly without its colorful wings—impaired but somehow still captivating even in her disadvantaged state.

Later that evening, Officers Fernandez and Smith passionately tongue kissed on the roof landing of 1809 Harmony Avenue, one of the more troublesome buildings in the precinct. This, as Lieutenant Garret and Cheddar approached the garbage-adorned vestibule of the same building to conduct a vertical patrol. While Fernandez was unzipping Smith's duty jacket, Rose was repeatedly punching the busted button for the thirty-ninth floor inside the urine-stained elevator of the adjacent monstrosity, *1805* Harmony Avenue. Rose revealed disgust at yellowing supermarket circulars on the ground as an elderly woman held tightly to the blue rosary around her neck while pinching her nostrils in defense of her olfactory senses with her other hand.

Garret and Cheddar had chosen to ascend their hazardous edifice via the squalid "A" staircase, in search of potential robbers or rapists hiding in the darkness of certain landings with non-working lights. Their flashlights gleamed streams of light, which angled off walls and splintered through the balusters that supported saliva-soiled handrails. An amorous sound grew more and more identifiable the closer the two got to the roof. A loud moan could be heard from there, just as a loud *thump* could be heard when Rose kicked the life out of the roof door and punched his firearm out in front of him in anticipation of any adversaries waiting to ambush him.

Simultaneously, at 1809 Harmony Avenue, an out-of-breath Lieutenant Garret and Cheddar finally arrived at the high point of the building and their night. The two shook off the lactic acid in their heavying legs and—after pausing to catch their breath—confirmed that they were ready via a mutual head nod. Garret delivered a super-kick to the roof door as the security alarm wailed with great disturbance at the night.

"Oh fuck!" ejaculated Fernandez, interrupted mid-act with no place to seek cover.

"Police, don't move!" announced the lieutenant and his driver in unison before Cheddar broke character and began taking in Smith's splendid, hairless, mostly naked body.

"Holy shit," he marveled, as Fernandez reminded Cheddar not to shoot him, considering his gun was still pointed at the two imperiled paramours. Smith was bent over on two stacked milk crates. Both of their pants were bunched around their ankles and Smith's supple breasts jiggled from her duty jacket as they overhung past the "Dairy Farms" logo of the top milk crate. The detail and literalness of her breasts actually being milky was not lost on Cheddar, who consumed every little inch of Smith as if through a straw with his already beady eyes bulging. He scanned her thoroughly, dropping his line of sight to her southern hemisphere.

"*Ho. Ly. Shit.* She has the *bald eagle*," Cheddar blurted as a mortified Smith scrambled to put her uniform back on. Fernandez stood there wearing nothing below his belt line, trying to explain what was unmistakably and transparently transpiring to an irate and disturbed Garret.

"Put your fucking *cock* away!" Garret ordered at the height of his yelling capabilities.

"Yeah, wrap that thing around your waist or something. Are you by any chance half-black?" Cheddar delivered with a comedian's charisma as the lieutenant ordered his driver to shut his salivating mouth.

"I make you the fucking training officer and this is how you thank me? I saved your ass when they wanted to transfer you to the seven-five, Noel!"

"I know, Lieu'. I'm sorry, sir! I promise—"

"You promise nothing! Because I'm transferring your ungrateful ass to Bronx Central Booking." Garret turned his ire to Smith who was now cowering and sniffling under the shame of her actions. She zipped up her NYPD jacket and stared at the tips of her boots as eye contact with anybody at this point was far too demeaning.

"And you, young lady: *house mouse* from now on! You're answering phones at the precinct until you can learn to keep your legs closed at work. Whatta' ya' got, five minutes on the job? It's too soon for this type of shit. Am I running a precinct or an escort service?"

Garret asked this rhetorically, but Cheddar was more than willing to play court jester and throw a third option into play.

"Police porn: dark poles in pink holes," Cheddar rhymed, standing in the awkward air of his crass comment. The lack of a reaction by anyone coldly scolded him more than anyone actually could. Perhaps the cold air had further frozen his tact or just exposed his lack of couth and situational awareness. Subject two didn't really care and he spent that uncomfortable car ride to the precinct trying to make eye contact through the rear view mirror as the two ruined sweethearts sunk in the back seat like the lawbreakers they corral.

Back at 1805 Harmony Avenue, Rose climbed a short flight of steps that led into the elevator room. He paused, and then dramatically pulled open the door revealing a pile of the killers' blood-stained clothes. He shined his flashlight at the evidence and wore a smile that shone brighter than the portable light that he controlled firmly in his grip. Rose celebrated outwardly but then he ambled over to the ledge of the roof as just a hint of stress started to infiltrate his countenance. His boot crunched a beer can, which he picked up and auto-pitched to himself, batting it into the distance with his expandable baton. Rose removed his hat and admired the picture of Cecelia, which was tucked inside a small protective plastic square stitched into the inside crown of the eight-point cap. It had faded badly after the detective's prank. He angered, detesting the distance and time that separated him from his wife-to-be. She had left a huge vacancy in a life that was filled with vacancies already. He put the hat on, pulling down hard on the short brim, hiding his eyes from the world on that chilly, gravelly rooftop. This was one of the idiosyncrasies that had begun to stand out to me as I studied subject one. And it represented one of his most salient traits—defiance. Rose sat on the ledge now, his legs dangling and his boots clicking against red brick, staring out at the embattled Bronx *barrio* that he swore to protect. He was just a man and his thoughts, the moon serving as the lamp providing the necessary light to contemplate. Rose scrolled through the contacts on his phone and reached out to Cheddar, now back at the precinct, and who Rose had started to confide in slowly.

Cheddar's phone rumbled against the pen-graffitied imitation wood of the bench where he changed. His locker was plastered with Hello Kitty stickers on the outside—which covered up the department-issued Police Don't Move sticker—and nude centerfolds on the inside. He almost didn't answer his phone but finally did when he realized it was "P.O. Rosebud," as he had saved it.

"E-Harmony, how can I hook you up?"

"Giselle was telling the truth!" Rose erupted.

"What? You're still talking to that little tramp? Let that go, man," dismissed a disinterested Cheddar, observing a shamed Fernandez reluctantly clearing out his locker ahead of his imminent transfer.

"No, listen! I found the bloody clothes that the perps ditched. They *have* to match the blood samples collected by Crime Scene," Rose explained, trying to convince Cheddar of his triumph.

"Listen to me, Rose. You're a nice guy and I like you a lot. You're a cool dude, but you're no damn detective. The ME's office isn't gonna release any information to you. You have to be debriefed by the detective squad as to how you even got that lead. What are you going to say, 'My little girlfriend told me?' Quit while you're ahead. I'm telling you: don't play with fire if you're not ready for skin grafts."

"Graft your ass. I'm using her. I'm going to keep milking the girl."

"That's a very poor choice of words," reprimanded a quickening Cheddar.

"I know. I just caught that," Rose acquiesced. "But she has the information I need. She's my ticket to the gold shield."

"Your ticket to jail is more like it. Follow procedure, Matlock," advised Cheddar, his accent more perceivable now as he slightly mispronounced the name.

"*Matlock*, not *mutlack*, was an attorney you fool. And I didn't even know they broadcasted American television in the dingy, bread-filled tents of Yugoslavia."

"I'm Albanian, asshole. And although I sound like an immigrant, I've still seen enough episodes of young Sherlock Holmes to know that you ain't no sleuth."

"But you are a *sloth*. I don't know why I even bothered to call you. I hope you pulled a body out of Harmony Avenue today to justify your employment with the NYPD."

"What?" Cheddar asked, "I got a body alr—" just as Rose abruptly hung up the phone on him. Cheddar would not give Rose the moral sanction that he, for some reason, sought from him. And so Rose pocketed his phone and surveyed the rooftop one last time.

Rose permitted the stars to look down on him, through the contaminated, eggplant-colored Bronx haze. He opened up to them and hoped that they would favor him in his quest, which was becoming more patently outlined now. The night slowly faded and the scarce stars dimmed and then stopped twinkling altogether and a new day ultimately revealed itself from the deep darkness of that deeply revelatory night. I courteously asked my commanding officer to remove me from the investigation at this point, experience predictively informing me that this could all play out in less than commemorative fashion. But he rejected my request and instead handed me a blue and yellow city pass for the Empire State Building and a blank overtime slip with his signature already scribbled on it. And so I mentally prepared myself for an early, exhilarating morning—the potential for scandal real—in the throbbing heart of hustling Midtown Manhattan.

Chapter V

On the morning of their first coordinated rendezvous, the Empire State Building marched right up to the lip of the freshly-awoken azure sky and gave it a good morning kiss. Clouds sveltely swam in and scratched their backs against its sun-warmed spire as it stood at attention and waited for the arrival of Officer Rose and his aspiring snitch. The two met at the shoelace of the slender, iconic New York citizen and locked eyes the way a locomotive fastens to the car that it pulls by a greasy coupler. They had both cleaned up beautifully, stepping into the moment with the very best versions of themselves on this, the first day of their lily pad leap into working in collusion with one another.

"Look at you," Giselle admired, "a regular GQ model. What's that, Dolce and Gabbana?"

"On my salary? Right. Macy's sales rack—no returns. You look amazing. Like somebody right out of *Sex in the City*."

"*Sex In the City?* That can be arranged," Giselle twisted.

"What did I tell you about that?" Rose scolded.

"I'm sorry but the name of the show is *Sex and the City*."

Rose walked up to a shabby looking security guard and displayed his NYPD badge. The guard nodded his head and made a sweeping motion with his hand, guiding Rose in. Giselle wore an "I told you so" kind of smile as they glided toward the revolving doors. Rose entered a compartment and leaned on the push-bar as Giselle comically squeezed into the same slot as him at the very last second. The door jammed momentarily before it resumed rotating and Rose and Giselle spilled out on the other side. They both looked up and took in the majesty of the 102-story building's golden atrium with its art deco lines and angles welcoming the pair, wrapping them up in its illustrious aura.

Rose took two short steps, Giselle followed closely. He took two more and Giselle clipped the heel of his freshly-polished Oxfords which were carefully selected, along with the rest of his ensemble, for this afternoon's rooftop conference. The two approach a second, saltier security guard.

"How many?" the guard asked disinterestedly.

"Just two. Me and my . . . um, my cousin here," Rose mumbled.

"Oh baby!" Giselle erupted. "You're going to propose to me up there aren't you? Just like I always dreamed. You're so romantic, baby!"

Rose wore a mask of mortification. The guard funneled them through two chrome, velvet-roped stanchions and pointed them in the direction of a rising escalator.

"Yeah, she's not well, sir, Tourette syndrome," Rose explained, he himself developing a tic of looking over his shoulder now.

"Hey, I ain't judging you, boss. A hot piece of ass like that? I won't tell nobody. I ain't IAB or nothing like that," the guard stated as Giselle subtly drifted away from this awkward exchange and toward the machinery of the moving staircase.

"Who said anything about internal affairs?" Rose paused, with hints of guilt and suspicion flavoring the question. "But seriously, man, she's only sixteen. She's not my girl, so don't say that."

"Look, I'm the same as you, boss. If there's grass in the field, I'm playing ball. You know what I mean?"

"Oh I see: if she's old enough to crawl, she's already in the right position? That sort of thing?" Rose asked with disgust for the grungy guard growing in his voice. The square badge affirmed this as Rose dismissed him and counterintuitively reached for Giselle's hand—bent exaggeratedly at the wrist—her fingers fluttering impatiently for him.

Moments later, the two were experiencing the outdoor eighty-sixth floor observation deck. A spirited wind howled as it skated over icy New York and pushed Giselle and Rose closer together. Giselle didn't miss this moment to rest her head on the young cop's shoulder. Rose squirmed at this, but held the uneasy position.

"Thank you for bringing me here, honey," Giselle manipulated.

"I'm not your honey," Rose corrected. "I'm here under duress. Gun to my head basically."

"Don't say that if it isn't true. You wanted to come up here with me. And wouldn't you say the view is magnificent?"

Rose just nodded. He sought to escape but there was no route marked at this precise moment.

"Would you like to maybe use some words right now?" Giselle suggested.

"Not necessarily."

"I'll even help you: say an adjective," Giselle persisted.

"*Irritating*," Rose offered, shooing Giselle away with his fly swatter-like tone.

"I don't like that one. Perhaps we can be more positive. . . Hey, I never asked you: are you married?"

"Engaged."

"To who?"

"Not to you!" Rose exclaimed, imitating a volcano. "Never gonna happen so you can forget that little stunt you pulled downstairs."

"I was just playing, love," Giselle lobbed nonchalantly, leaving the word "love" in the air just long enough for Rose to bite on it.

"Don't call me 'love'. You gotta stop playing, and I mean like *yesterday*. I can get jammed up over something like that. I'm here because you were right about the elevator shaft but don't get this twisted. This isn't a date," Rose clarified, expressing a notion that he was perhaps convincing himself of too.

"This is whatever I want it to be," Giselle bottom-lined, stunning and angering Rose simultaneously.

"You must be smoking the same crack your boys are selling," Rose shot back. "That's some good shit because you are *twisted*," he stated, twisting the knife and shriveling Giselle, in the process reclaiming the power from her.

Rose had allowed her to wield it for an extended period, but he took this moment to illustrate that he had been playing nice and certainly had more facets to him than he had, up until now, revealed. Giselle appeared to be affected by this shift and she aloofly turned her back to him.

"Hey, I'm sorry. I didn't think you were so sensitive. Maybe that was harsh, but it's just that you have to understand . . ."

"Understand what? That we can't have a sexual relationship? No shit, Aristotle, I was just flirting."

"Well, maybe you need to stop flirting, *Plato*. Maybe you need to filter your discourse a bit and recognize the danger of this situation. We can both get in serious trouble for even being up here. And you can get *hurt*."

"I'm already hurt, or can't you tell?" Giselle asked, knowing full well that she wore the pain that life inflicted on her the way most people wear a scarf. It wrapped around her neck, knotted at her skinny throat and restricting her, as Rose unwittingly tried to loosen it.

"I can tell actually. And I feel really bad about that."

Rose felt the rock shifting underneath the sole of his foot but he wasn't ready to slip just yet.

"So tell me, who did those clothes belong to? Who actually committed those murders on Ash Wednesday? I need names. I need addresses. I need—"

"You need, you need, you need," Giselle complained. "Why in the hell should I tell you? What do I get from helping you reach your goal? You get your promotion and I get what, fucked some more? I'm sore enough as it is."

"Listen, if I make detective I can put you on the payroll. I can make you my confidential informant, pay you a decent salary and we can solve big crimes together. Once I realize my dream, it opens up avenues for you to improve your circumstances."

"Oh, *your* dreams? Well, what about my nightmares? When you get your big promotion and they move you to a better precinct, you'll discard me like a used condom. I know. It's happened before. And what's the big deal about making detective? I see a bunch of them sniffing around for clues hating their lives. Why is it so important for you to get that little gold shitty shield?" She was becoming more emotional and this attracted empathy from Rose, who picked a peculiar path to a connection.

"Because my hero was a detective. Some people idolize ballplayers or actors. You probably idolize a stripper or something. Well, I grew up idolizing a detective," Rose revealed, sneaking in a jab while visibly uncomfortable with the intimate subject matter.

"What was his name? This detective?" Giselle continued, sensing that she was venturing into some new, poignant territory.

"You ask a lot of freaking questions!" Rose shouted, calling attention to the pair.

"Well so do you," Giselle retaliated softly, bringing the tone back to hushed levels. "A name for a name. Give me his name and I'll give you a name."

"Rose—Detective Reinaldo Rose." He surrendered the eponym and felt a great weight come off his shoulders. It was the first time he had spoken his father's name aloud to anyone since joining the force. He paced about the crowding observation deck, uncertain if the interrogation had concluded.

"Respect," Giselle stated, lifting her hands in the air submissively. "Not knocking that. But don't they come in once it's too late? After the bloodbath? I mean wouldn't you rather be the one preventing the killings, like you do now?"

"Yeah, a lot of killings I prevent. Detectives solve the case. They take the perps off the streets so these baboons can't rob or rape anymore."

"Oh, it's baboons you want to lock up? I think I see the Central Park Zoo from here. I'm sure they have at least a couple of baboons there for you to bring in."

"Listen, if you're thinking I'm something, I'm not *that*. If someone kills an old lady or poisons the community with drugs, makes people unemployable, creates a culture of fear and intimidation through their horrific violence, then to me, they're animals—mutts. Excuse the zoology term, it's not politically correct, I know, but . . . it is what it is. Our mission is to preserve life by protecting the lives of the people in our communities. I actually care about them; I don't just say that I do. I'm not someone running for office, I'm an *officer*. . . At least until I get my gold shield," Rose caveated, almost as a postscript.

Giselle finally backed down. She excused herself from the conversation and simply took in the breathtaking panorama that stretched out before her.

"Wow. Look at that. Central Park looks like a huge green quilt laid down between an awesome canyon of concrete and steel," Giselle vividly captured.

"What was that? Say that again. Since when did you start getting all Emily Dickinson on me? Are you taking a poetry class or something?"

"You think that just because I'm a hood rat I can't express myself. Remember, I'm ghetto, not stupid."

"Hey, I'm not stigmatizing you."

"Sure you aren't. So now that you know I'm literate, can you hurry up and propose to me?" Rose shot a harpoon through Giselle's mammoth smile. "I'm kidding. Kidding dammit. You look like you want to throw me off the ledge. Bring it down ten notches."

"Okay, enough with the games. Are you ever going to give me anything substantial? I need more than cryptic clues and bloody sweatshirts. What exactly happened at '1805' that night? Was that a changing of the guard?" Rose pressed, inquisitively.

"I'll tell you—I will. But first you have to get through Puff and Jeff. They're the dealers. They're the ones who fuck your girl up." She amplified her sex appeal now. "If you want me as an ally, you have to take them out of the equation. But you'll need to catch them by surprise because they pack serious heat."

"I'm packing some serious heat too: Mr. Smith. I'll blow the lid off those goons and this case. And I'll get promoted for shutting down their entire operation."

"Okay, terminator. May I suggest you use stealth, not stupidity? Are you listening to your girl?" she questioned, her repetition of that phrase a simplistic attempt to ingrain it in Rose's mind.

Tourists bantered now and deposited their converted coins into telescopic apparatus used to view the grand city. The granite and glass summits, valleys, and plateaus were gazed at admiringly through the fogged magnifying lens. The city really allowed its personality to shine through that day. Its teeth—comprised of superabundant office windows—reflected the sunrays as the monuments smiled wide, toothy smiles. Lights of office lamps flickered on and off mystically, while venetian blinds flapped up and down, winking at finicky admirers, creating a kinetic city-citizen flirtation. Buildings exaggerated their heights, comparing themselves against their peers and adding a few stories by tiptoeing on their doormen-attended lobbies. Clusters of yellow cabs formed Tetris-like shapes and morphed to fit into tight spaces, blocking intersections as pedestrians cursed them and compared them to sewer-dwelling dung. The city sung its unique tune: clamorous car honks and booming jackhammers, rhythmic street performers and pulsating police sirens. Street vendors dished out *street meat* to the drumbeat down at crane city, all while Giselle melodically whispered secret key-like information into Rose's elated ear. He awoke at her revelation; he was galvanized by her bold decision to confidentially inform him.

"Holy shit!" Rose rejoiced. "No more *Blue's Clues*? No more *Da Vinci Code* history-based riddles? Is it my birthday or something?"

"Oh damn, I forgot the Ice cream cake. You like that right, though? *Declaration of Independence*, forty-first president? It keeps you on your toes, no?"

"Screw that! Bill of Rights, Pledge of Allegiance. If I would have paid attention in history class, I would have solved half the crimes in this precinct by now. You couldn't say *Paradise Lost* or *The Canterbury Tales*? Something I'm more familiar with."

"Um . . . I don't know those," Giselle admitted. "Maybe *The Great Gatsby* or *Catcher in the Rye* or something?"

"Wait, you know *The Catcher in the Rye*? You're kidding me, right?" Rose verified, realizing a bond was being forged against his better judgment. Giselle built the bridge.

"I'm in high school. Required reading. Plus, Holden Caulfield is sixteen—like me. We both got kicked out of school too. He's a badass. And I'm kinda' like a female version of him."

Rose smiled at this. He didn't even notice he was nodding his head in approval. He rushed to speak as his enthusiasm lead him now.

"That's my favorite book of all time! I mean, 'how do you know what you're going to do until you do it?'" Rose recited, still giddy at discussing his favorite novel.

"Oh, you're quoting it now?" Giselle exposed. "Would you like to write my book report for me? It was due—wait for it—last week!"

The two chuckled and giggled as if in a state of inebriation. They didn't realize this one commonality was disarming them both and bringing them harmoniously into duet.

"I would write that report in a heartbeat. And it would have to be off the top of my head because I actually lost my copy on the train one time. I fell asleep and next thing I know—"

"You got pickpocketed for your *Catcher in the Rye*?" Giselle interrupted, giggling some more. "Like seriously, I didn't know thieves were into literature like that. That sounds a little farfetched to me. It's probably *on* you right now." Giselle pretended to frisk Rose, patting him in places. She continued, "Doesn't every serial killer they find have a copy of that book on them? You aren't a serial killer are you? I'm not going to end up chopped up and mailed out to all the senators am I?"

"Maybe just the Republican ones," Rose quipped. "And a few governors maybe."

Giselle half-smiled at Rose and reached for the warmth of his body. He hesitated at first, before surrendering, placing his arm around her and pulling her into his physical core as she made gains on his emotional core. The wind howled now, trying to get noticed amidst the vociferous voice of New York City during its morning roar. Giselle was almost blown away by one particularly temperamental gust aiming to graduate to a gale. She was already airy herself as Rose's approving tone was ethereally lifting her out of her discount heels. She curled a little more into him like a little puppy curling its nose into its own warm fur. They were coalescing, even as Rose tried to keep them separate. Counterproductively, he rotated her body for her, and draped both of his arms around her shoulders. His chin rested at her crown and she wore it regally. She felt his heart beating against her back and relaxed her body into his. There was a certain ballet to the way they held their hands in unison. She was tucked into him as if he was about to unravel her with a climactic twirl. But she remained there, his willful prisoner. She wanted to extend the moment somehow, but instead she put a caption to it.

"Sometimes, something that people take for granted just captures you. It just holds you there like a newborn baby and you feel . . ."

"Loved?"

Rose did not intend to complete her sentence, but it happened. Suddenly, it was like he had opened up a museum in his heart and this memory with her was the first painting that would hang inside of it. He didn't know it yet, but he would amass an entire gallery of precious moments with Giselle. But on this day, he merely enjoyed the picture-perfection of their rooftop rendezvous. He felt energized but could feel dirt forming underneath his fingernails from the questionable proceedings. His heart was pure but something about the situation left him feeling soiled. Giselle and Rose breathed in clouds, which swirled through the air and into their deep inhales, filling their lungs with newly birthed life.

The city stirred and the Empire State Building preened against the mirrors of other, lesser-known structures. Tourists trampled over each other for a photo op against the skyline, which looked like the vertical zigzag pattern from the electrical impulses of an EKG. And the pair's heart activity surely fluctuated at this unexpected, romantic juncture. It was unclear how Giselle and Rose would unattach, but they *had* to. Giselle uncoiled from Rose's core and faced him again. Yes, she was a problem—this was unequivocal at this point—standing before him, so perfect in his eyes suddenly. Her flaws were starting to look like charms on a bracelet to him; they were little, diminutive amulets of character rather than reasons to stay away from her. He couldn't stay away from her if he tried at this point. Neither one of them could stop what was coming.

ENTR'ACTE

When Rose arrived home that afternoon, the first thing he did was pick up a picture of Cecelia and him at their happiest. Rose admired their synchronous smiles as he opened up a bottle of light, aromatic pinot noir. He reminisced on his morning atop the Empire State Building just as he put his cell phone to his ear to listen to a voicemail that his fiancée had left him.

"Hey baby, it's me. The love of your life . . ."

Rose flipped the cork into the air and slapped the oak out of it as Cecelia continued. "I thought you said you were off today, so I don't know why you aren't picking up your phone. I called you a *few* times. Anyway, I'm off to class now. I hope you're well. I love you. Talk tonight!"

Rose poured himself a glass of the California legend. A rich cherry-red wine swirled around the bulbous rim of his glass like a NASCAR leader roaring around the bend. It rode the rim before wobbling from side to side and eventually settling into his half-full glass. Or maybe it was half-empty. Rose leaned way the hell back in his black leather computer chair and exhaled loudly. He sat there, thinking deeply, sinking into a stinking hole—brinking on a sinkhole—while drinking west coast ambrosia from the Napa Valley. He sucked up the nectar, plucked from the plump black *Vitis* grape and inebriated to escape the dilemma which was clarifying before him. Rose drowsed following his daytime drink fest and closed his eyes to reality for the comforts of his dreams. He faded into the afternoon, awakening for brief spells and playing back moments of that altering afternoon in his wine-altered mind. It all blurred and it needed to blur because a clear picture was problematic for various reasons now.

Two days later, rain inhabited the air, plummeting down from darkening, nefarious nimbostratus clouds. At their contraband cave, Puff and Greer played videogames as drugs rested messily on a faux marble table counter. Thunder erupted and lightning struck down with unbolted rage at the night. In the fifty-first precinct, Rose and Cheddar place down their own videogame controllers and rose up purposefully. Rain tap-danced on the window sill, its percussion creating the beat to which the beasts would dance on this night of crime noir. Cinematic showers began to pound down on this South Bronx slum. Nature provided the rhythm of intense pitter-patter—like a boxer hitting the mitts—as the streets were cleansed of blood, booze, and semen. Rose and Cheddar guided along a short concrete path underneath a red brick building on an avenue named "Prospect" but possessing no such hope. Enormous rats scurried, squeaked, and squealed their way over mountains of rank-smelling garbage bags in this dank alley. Rose scaled a chain link fence, his gangly partner following his lead. Rose then leapt up and gripped a rusted fire escape ladder, pulling it down for the athletically-challenged Cheddar. They ascended the wet, slippery steps to the rooftop and traversed the minefield of syringe needles embedded in the gravel before pulling open the door to the roof landing. The duo descended the staircase, stepping over chicken bones and slimy condoms, which were residually strewn on the ground. Graffiti read: "N.Y.P.D: NEW YORK'S PUSSY DEPARTMENT." Rose made the sign of the cross as he and Cheddar arrived at the first floor landing. They leapt together, taking flight, parachuting into a war, unbeknownst to them at that very moment.

"Police, put your hands up!" Rose yelled, as Puff and Greer turned to stone. Greer dropped a bag of fresh reefer as Puff released his Hennessy bottle. Glass smashed against white and black tiles as corrupt aromas filled the air and the busted drug dealers eyed an escape route.

"Move and I'll put a bullet in your ass. Hands where I can see them," Cheddar commanded.

Rose searched the two arrestees, recovering over one hundred bags of marijuana from pockets within pockets. He checked the nearby mailboxes and discovered stashed drugs, in bulk.

"The tip was good. Special delivery," Rose wisecracked. "Put your hands behind your back, the both of you."

"That shit ain't mine," Greer claimed.

"No, it's the fucking postman's," Rose rebutted.

Greer glanced over his shoulder and read Rose's nameplate and badge number. Rose handcuffed his prisoners as Cheddar cautiously covered them with his service weapon.

"We're already cuffed. Game over, right?" Puff asked. "Why don't you put your gun away, you scared or something? The last thing you want to do is shoot an unarmed black man, white boy."

"Shut up, mope," Cheddar ordered.

"She fucked up again," Greer muttered through clenched, cognac-stained teeth.

"What did you just say?" Rose asked, excitedly.

"He said a little slut fucked up. Do you know her?" Puff investigated, venturing to steal a glimpse at Rose's cards.

"Be careful what you say. You take me to that place and my baton will be all over your crack-storing ass," Rose alerted.

"Oh, so you are a faggot?" Greer antagonized. "I bet you fantasize about putting your shit in my ass."

"Watch your mouth," Rose warned, his face altered by repulsion.

"Watch *yours*," threatened an emboldened Greer before cracking open Rose's mouth with a vicious head-butt. Rose saw stars and cocked his fist back to deliver vengeance. But instead of retaliating he savored the metallic tang in his mouth before ejecting out a stream of saliva-mixed life juice. He cocked his fist back a second time as the manacled perpetrator braced his body for impact. Rose resisted the cathartic violence of pummeling Greer, as a crimson-toothed smile unfurled across his roseate face.

"Those cuffs saved you, punk! Now I can add 'assault on a PO' to your charges, asshole. And that is exactly why you're a dumb-ass, low-life perp, piece of shit perp."

Rose was a bit shaken by this attack. He brought his hand—slightly shaking from anger—to his lips and examined his bloody fingertips. He gathered himself and affirmed his position competitively before he and Cheddar escorted the fettered felons out of the premises to await transportation back to the base.

These arrests were symbolic, as the first step in the ad hoc plan that Giselle had outlined for him was now successfully completed. Bringing in her misusers was the equivalent of putting a "w" up on an imaginary scoreboard and the significance of this was not lost on the tenacious, cerebral Rose, who began carving out a path to the gold shield the minute Giselle opened up to him from her literal position on the ground on the afternoon of their introduction. But the plan needed a catalyst, and that's exactly what it received once the first bullet ripped through the well-worn fiber of that bloody Ash Wednesday night in the Bronx. And Rose was the vehicle, and the conductor, singularly steering it—in runaway fashion—along with his destiny; he was going after his ambitions with an indefatigable zeal that was equal parts precocious and perilous, but was now as intrinsic a part of his being as any of the petals and thorns that constituted him.

CHAPTER VI

Later that evening at the precinct, Rose rode the toilet bowl and reflected inwardly with a tri-folded piece of a napkin tucked into the inside of his broken lip. He traced the cop art scribbled on the wall with his intense eyes. "Sgt. Sanchez sucks big bull cock" and "Lt. Garret swallows" were among the amusing adornments but "P.I.F.L.: patrol is for losers" is the one that made Rose chuckle. That is until banging on the stall door interrupted his serene moment of introspection.

"Ay yo' kid, you gotta go upstairs and watch your perps. You can't just hide down here," shouted Officer Fable, performing his role as stationhouse security guard with fervent enthusiasm.

"Hey big guy, if it's all the same to you, I'd like to finish wiping my ass. Are you cool with that?" Rose asked rhetorically.

"Wipe your ass, rub one out, I don't give a shit kid. But if sarge has to come down here looking for you, you're gonna be fucked."

"What, I'm gonna get a foot post again?" Rose quipped, right before flushing the toilet over the senior officer's response. "Hey, is it true that Sergeant Sanchez sucks big bull cock?" Rose queried with a smile, before dashing up the stairs to see what all the fuss was about.

This was happening just as Kilo and Diablo admired massive drug profits stacked toweringly at a round glass table inside their smoke-filled stash house. The opaque tendrils rose from the sticky roaches that they drew from, granulating into the air before being dissipated altogether by lazily rotating paddles.

"Puff and Greer got locked up tonight," informed a stoic Diablo, rattling the wood and brass dominoes segregated away from the money on the table.

"They got caught with a nice amount. They hit the cop too."

"Those guys are idiots," chimed Kilo. "Who was looking out, it had to be Giselle, right?"

"It was Giselle. But don't worry about it. I'll address the situation," assured Diablo, as the darkness of night swaddled the restless town and slowly rocked it to sleep.

Rose however, did not sleep. He stirred at the precinct, shuffling his arrest paperwork from one workstation to another. He pecked away at clicking typewriter keys, trying to piece together a property voucher for the arrest evidence. Rose ultimately finished his paperwork and interrupted Sergeant Valdez's hellacious game of Tetris on her now outmoded flip phone.

"Sarge, were you looking for me?"

"Yeah—hours ago. Where the hell have you been hiding? And what did you think, those mutts in the cells were going to transport themselves?"

"No, ma'am, I was just wrapping up the invoices and was going to ask—"

"Forget about it. I got two do-nothings to go instead. If you're finished with your paperwork, you can leave. You'll be right back here in no time anyway," reminded the impact sergeant as Rose checked the clock on the wall distrustfully. He made his way downstairs to change before his lonely gypsy cab ride home.

Prior to collapsing into his bed, Rose set the alarm clock at his nightstand—the interlaced cup ring marks having grown in number—for twelve noon. He plowed into a cluster of pillows and closed his eyes for what seemed like seconds before the screech of his alarm clock plowed into his pillowy dreams, pushing reality out at the sides. Rose slammed his hand against his mattress, angry at so much now. He was unrested and un-rejuvenated and began to whirlpool around in his cluttered mind everything that was transpiring in his disarranged life.

At 5:15 p.m., Rose death-walked into the precinct muster room with a short form in his left hand. He felt incomplete from again missing his daily conversation with Cecelia and pressure had started to build in the network of pipes that comprised him. He requested Lieutenant Garret's ear.

"Sure, I have a minute for you," Garret consented. "By the way, great collar last night. Is your lip alright though?"

"It's nothing, boss. Occupational hazard. I'm fine. I just need you to sign my 'twenty-eight' for my vacation."

"Taking time off so soon, are you?" the lieutenant asked. "Matter of fact, let me get that—done. Forget about this place for a while. But when you return, I want more of these great collars."

"Oh, I'm working on something big," Rose revealed. "I'm talking gun collars, *plural*."

"That's my boy! Rookie superstar. Your father would be proud," Garret assessed encouragingly.

The effect of that last line was as if someone had completely disrobed Rose the way a magician whips a sheet off a table setting during his tablecloth trick. Everything was still mostly intact but he felt completely naked. Rose stood there, motionless and carrying blankness on his face, certain that he had denied his relation to Detective Rose in a prior conversation.

"Attention to roll call!" sounded Garret.

As scrambling rookies bumped into Rose, he somehow was pushed into the formation, still stunned. Rose thought about his father as his eyes collected water. He lowered his head to hide his brown orbs under the rim of his eight-point hat but then the tears welled up, threatening to overflow. He tilted his chin up and spread the moisture in his eyes out over his cornea creating miniature pools. His eyelashes absorbed his sadness, and then he fixated on a bank robbery informational wanted poster. It read: "Wanted: Two male blacks, black masks, black firearms. Stated "don't be a hero," demanded fifties and hundreds." Garret paused for effect and began his roll call speech.

"I want to tell you guys something. Forget about the color and return date for now. Yesterday, two officers missed getting into a shootout with bank robbers by about thirty seconds. Surveillance cameras caught the perps' faces and you know what else they caught? The cops walking into the bank talking on their cell phones. They thought the job was bullshit. Half a minute earlier and their last words would have been "I'll call you back." The rookies laughed at this.

"It's not funny!" scolded Garret. "*Complacency*! Complacency kills. We die on this job when we relax. One day, you're going to turn the corner on your foot post and two guys are going to be holding up a liquor store with Glocks."

Rose sobbed into his jacket. He tasted his own tears as Garret's speech picked up its intensity and momentum.

"What are you going to do, spray and pray? This is life and death out here. In this gun battle, second place is a body bag; we're the police, we *have* to win! God forbid the shit hits the fan the fight doesn't end when you get shot—it just begins. You did not come on to this job to die in some filthy gutter in the Bronx. I don't care what anybody says, dying doesn't make you a hero; it only makes you a corpse. We deal with the worst first. Tag, you're *it*. But if you shoot at me I'm shooting back. If you are ever in that situation, you take their life. You take the life of the person who's trying to take yours. Dispatch those motherfuckers to hell and let the devil deal with them!"

The impact lieutenant exited the room after deeply impacting his subordinates. Rose hid in the plainness of sight, piecing himself back together slowly. He would flutter in place for a while before regaining use of his legs and making his way out into the warm comforts of the cold, like a boxer making it back to his corner after barely avoiding getting knocked out. He needed someone to splash water on his face as he was totally punch drunk at this time, but there were no detectives in sight.

Outside, snowflakes the size of corn flakes began to flutter briskly through the crisp air. School children in colorful coats and scarves caught the powdery white ice clusters on their tongues, melting its six-fold symmetry. On various street corners, drug dealers exchanged packaged white powder for the new green and blue twenty dollar bills. By a garbage dumpster, a Hispanic male penetrated a Catholic school girl, still in her green and blue plaid skirt, from behind. A church organ *gonged*, inviting believers into the House of God. In the church, light fought its way through gorgeous stained glass windows as a stark white statue of the Virgin Mary glowed from the flames of surrounding candles. Christ hung off a crucifix, still bleeding for our sins, and the gold and red tabernacle concealed the Eucharist. The entire timeline that, when reversed, is transubstantiation was present on that altar like the world's fastest time lapse display. Hands placed tithe money into mesh baskets as cash and envelopes amassed. From their pews, churchgoers turned their heads toward the heavy oak doors which opened inwardly as snow blew, uninvited, into the mass. Rose knelt there, seeking the Lord's blessing, as the congregation sang *Hallelujah* at the priest's hymn. Rose dipped his fingertips into the tepid holy water, genuflected again and walked out of the church, pulling the oak doors behind him. He strode out to post where Giselle would intercept him as per their adopted convention.

"Solo foot post *again*?" she asked, enticed as ever by the intimate access that this granted her.

"My partner is driving the lieutenant again. Oh shit," Rose commented, noticing the black olive colored shades and Yankees cap that Giselle hid behind. "Witness protection program?"

"I might need it. Puff called me today. He said they should both be out soon."

"So you can just assault a cop and be back out on the streets in no time? Some criminal justice system we have," Rose commented angrily.

"My guess is they gave somebody up," Giselle presumed, confidently.

"I know how it works," snapped Rose. "I guess I'll just have to collar those perps again. Do they suspect you informed?"

"That I *snitched*?" Giselle vernacularized. "No—I mean, I hope not. If they do, and Diablo and Kilo find out, I'm a goner. They'll order my death. Are you going to bring flowers to my funeral?"

"If anything happens to you, there's going to be a whole lot of funerals," Rose declared, mixing equal parts bravado and affection. "You're in my hands now. *I'm* protecting you."

It was apparent through this interaction that she had gained substantial purchase on his heart. Rose had somehow gotten caught up in Giselle's rip tide and was being pulled out into an ocean in which he couldn't possibly stay afloat. There was no life vest and no lighthouse in sight, just Rose trying to put a human face on policing and following the current of his insoluble emotions.

"Really? You really mean that Mr. *Man on Fire* over there?" Giselle attempted to confirm, basking in the upgraded status that she seemed to enjoy now.

"I do. Just call me 'Creasy'."

"'Creasy *bear*'," Giselle revised sentimentally, coloring in the outline. She smiled flirtatiously at Rose as the thermometer began to rise ever so slightly. He accepted her smile and reciprocated one back to her, wrapped in subtle apprehensiveness. They were joined in an unfurling moment. She sought to move the needle.

"You know," Giselle aroused, "I'm really starting to feel like now is the right time for me to reveal the identities of the Ash Wednesday killers to you."

"Is that a fact?" Rose questioned, his smile now evolving into a beaming grin, which he failed to fight back. His mission was brought back completely into focus. "And you're sure you want to do this, you're ready now?"

"Not *now*. But soon. After Tavern on the Green. I've read up on it: 'a romantic icon of the city tucked away in the bucolic crown jewel of New York.' It's supposed to be a five-star joint."

"I can't afford a five-star joint," Rose reminded, insecurely.

"So maybe you can afford to cook for me at your place," she explored, provocatively.

"Tavern on the green it is. Even if it's going to cost me about one month's salary," Rose exaggerated.

"So make it last a lifetime. Like those diamond commercials I see on television. I'm giving you gold. I'm giving you the identity of the murderers.

You can finally get that shield you've been talking about. That's priceless to you, right?"

"You're priceless," Rose blurted, realizing in an instant that he had slipped. He couldn't take it back now and perhaps, perchance it was a revelatory mandate at this point. It seemed to be becoming more and more evident that enough pieces on the board had been manipulated by fate and something that was once nothing more than a raging romanticization was shaping into their plausible reality. She believed—and that's what mattered—that at this precise moment she was indeed priceless to him and she used the capital she had just earned to leap into his arms. There's a way you go into someone's arms when you belong to them. She went in that way for the first time. He caught her and then placed her down—immediately— trying to regain control of the slippery steering wheel attached to his life by a suddenly rickety steering column. The air was so brisk now, and this *thing* before them invigorated them both.

"Once we do this, once I know who these guys are and where to find them, there's no turning back."

"And who would ever want to turn back?" Giselle replied trustingly.

"Well, it's too late anyway," Rose finalized, both of them understanding that their relationship had passed a certain threshold and now operated on a more substantive level. She was still only at the atrium of his heart, but was descending deeper into chambers where oxygen is in rich supply and yet it is still harder to sustain breath. This is because, for some reason, when love is born between two people it always becomes more difficult to breathe. They weren't quite there yet, or perhaps Rose wasn't. Giselle was starting to believe in her gravity's ability to pull Rose, hoping that the precarious way that they orbited around each other would lead to her crash landing and splashing into the ocean of his heart.

They separated and Giselle once again camouflaged into her decaying urban landscape. Rose swayed into the breeze and checked the calibration of his moral instruments. He was affected, and imbued with the green hues of optimism, willingly surrendering to Giselle the reciprocity that she had begged for.

Officers Jade and Fable pulled up next to him in their dirty blue and white police car, mugging Rose of the moment. Rose inspected their vehicle.

"Get in," ordered Jade.

"Get in?"

"Get in!" he reiterated, banging on the side of the vehicle through his lowered passenger side window. Rose squeezed into the back timidly, hitting his knees against the metal partition. He hastily scrawled a quick entry of this ride into his memo book.

"Guys, thank you but I don't go 'sixty-three' until twenty-three hundred hours. If the *lieu* comes around for a scratch and I'm off post—"

"Man, fuck the *lieu*," interjected a disgruntled Fable. "He's back at the house jerking off, watching the Knicks lose again. It's cold out here. You want your nuts to freeze? Back in the day we knew where to hide. Don't you know a good cop never gets cold, wet, or hungry?"

"I might have heard that somewhere," admitted Rose, nervously. "Are you guys doing a sector tonight? I can't wait to go into car."

"No, we're the senior guys on this tour. Sarge gave us a conditions auto thinking we would write a few summonses. We ain't writing shit. And we ain't fighting shit but time," disclosed Fable.

"Oh, I get it. Fighting crime, fighting time," Rose minimized, accentuating the rhyme.

"You're really sharp, *rook*," Fable mocked. "But what you don't realize is that while you were still shitting your diapers, we were fighting *real* violent crime in a city that you will never know. The year I came on the job, twelve cops were killed in the line of duty. That's one a month in case math isn't your best subject. I've been in the trenches since the *Seventies*; I've been there, I've done that. Now, we just try to make it through the night. Eight hours, thirty-five minutes. If you can do that for twenty years—because you'd be crazy if you stay longer—then you can retire with a healthy pension and get a bullshit job at a pharmacy or something. Be one of those square badges with your gut hanging over your dick."

"You know it's funny," Rose framed, "most security guards, they really, really wanted to be cops. And then most cops, it seems like they just really want to be security guards."

"Wow, you're a fucking genius, Rose," marveled Jade. "With insight like that, you must want to be a rocket scientist."

"Actually a detective," corrected Rose, somewhat snobbishly, which was out of character.

"Now why on earth would you want to be a goddamn detective? Is it because of your *dad*?" asked Jade, fortunate that the partition prevented Rose from knee-jerk punching him in the back of the head.

"What? *What?* My dad? Did you know him or something?"

"Detective Reinaldo Rose? What did you think, nobody would find out? He was the toughest son of a bitch in the South Bronx. Fearless. He made that gold shield mean something. Mean everything really," revealed Jade much to his passenger's amazement.

"Maybe," Rose managed. "Maybe my dad does have something to do with it. Maybe it is because of him that I want to apprehend real, vicious criminals and build a case and stick a knife right through their cold *fucking* hearts. I mean, from a justice standpoint," he clarified.

"Oh, of course. Justice," repeated Fable. "Because I was about to say if you want to stick a knife through someone's heart, you're probably on the wrong side of the law. That shit don't fly anymore. Back then, cops were kings. Now, we're garbage men. Just pick up the trash and you'll be fine."

"I didn't come on this job to pick up trash. I came here to help people. I came here to save people's lives. Call me an idealist or even stupid, but I'm here to make a difference—oh what the hell is this?" asked Rose, interrupting himself.

A commotion had erupted and sloshed bar patrons, a few misplaced thugs, and two aggressors violently spilled out of a popular watering hole. The two men pounded an Asian male until he crumbled feebly to the curbside, stomping on him while he was prone.

Rose and Jade practically fell out of their patrol car seats and rushed over to the offenders, while Fable parked. Jade slammed one of the combatants onto the hood of a double parked car. Rose placed his hand on the victim's shoulder and soothed him with rehearsed calm, reassuring words.

"Hey mister. Hey, we're gonna get an ambulance over here immediately, just stay with me." The injured male spat out a large clump of blood. Jade quickly handcuffed the man he manhandled. A second inebriated pugilist excitedly intervened.

"Hey guys! He's on the job. I'm on the job. We're both on the job!" disclosed the tipsy brawler, protesting the treatment of a man alleged to be their brother in blue.

"What are you talking about," asked Jade.

"We're cops. Just like you," the man clarified, pulling out a brilliant gold lieutenant's shield from his pocket. "This guy was acting like an asshole."

"Oh fuck," they appeared to say collectively, as Rose ripped off the tail of his uniform shirt to staunch the victim's bleeding.

"And what's this dude's deal?" Fable asked, entering the fold and controlling the handcuffed drunk by the chain links.

"Go ahead and check his pocket," offered the off-duty supervisor. And when Fable reached into the man's jeans and pulled out a gold captain's shield, all parties collectively understood which way this situation would be handled. Except, of course, Rose.

"Guys, should I raise up Lieutenant Garret over the air?"

"Are you fucking kidding me, rook!" exclaimed Jade. "That son of a bitch is shaky as hell. He'll call the duty captain and we'll all be jammed up. These guys are big *bosses*. They'll make your life a living hell. I don't see no crime here."

Jade uncuffed the off-duty captain, never actually obtaining his name. The off-duty lieutenant gave the two veterans a chummy pat on the back and stabbed Rose in the eye with a glare of disdain. The two emancipated boozers doddered off into the invisible horizon of the shadow-filled night, as the crowd ogred into obstreperousness. The angry faces in the now-unruly mass remolded, resembling grotesque gargoyles organized to converge on the embattled officers on the scene. Rose's face also morphed demonically as he wore the most incredulous of looks, holding up the victim's head with two hands like a church offering, while kneeling in a gutter. Rose examined the victim's blood, dripping down in between his trembling fingers. It was a deep crimson, enhanced by the cruel illumination of the moon. He impatiently waited for an ambulance, *wheeeyo-wheeyo'ing* in the distance, and his hands now acted as a spout carrying the stream of blood from a fractured skull into the sewer drain. It was a sickening red, the reddest red. That deep crimson color which saturates so many crime scenes and we've seen dispensed out so often from the cracked palette in this beautiful, horrible tale.

Chapter VII

At Tavern on the Green, a rich, red wine was poured by a handsome aspiring actor into a graceful Bordeaux glass. Champagne flutes clinked almost musically as patrons toasted to a hungerless life high atop the well-fed hog. They ate steaks as thick as mattresses and debated on the MOMA versus the Guggenheim with livelier than expected fervor. Another waiter delivered artistically-arranged food, sashaying through tables as the chandeliers in the restaurant reflected off his charismatic smile. Rose and Giselle entered together like one half-tuxedoed, half ball-gowned pretzel—arm in arm and walking as if their bodies were synchronized. Their entrance was an introduction, and they were framed perfectly by the cluster of consumers waiting to be seated and who parted for them as if they were Gatsby and Daisy. "Table for two," requested Giselle with Academy Award-worthy confidence. On this night, she looked utterly angelic. Her classy updo disguised her classless upbringing. She balanced herself on heels that she bedazzled herself using a glue stick as she herself remained glued together and bedazzled her audience. She was no longer the hood rat; she was a goddess divine and stole breaths as she postured in front of the maître d'. Rose stood upright, making every line in his suit visible and separate. The way it fit looked curiously couture for a struggling cop. His tie bore an exquisite line pattern and his hair was gelled perfectly, styled to the back, to keep the overall geometry of his appearance homogeneous.

"Call the cops. Grand larceny: somebody just stole my heart," Giselle stated through a shimmering smile that stretched the vertical lines on her lips to their labial limit.

"Why? They won't respond in time," replied Rose, fixating on the tiny lipstick stains on her teeth and the necklace that explored her diving neckline, which partially exposed two taut, tennis ball-sized breasts. Giselle's diamond-like nipples threatened to pierce the bust of her dress and unintentionally pointed the way to their seats. The hostess escorted them and Rose pulled out Giselle's chair, situating the young lady in what might as well have been a throne to her. Giselle instantly began playing with the silverware as Rose settled into the vantage point from which he would view Giselle for the majority of the night. She fidgeted mightily in her mighty chair.

"Relax," Rose instructed comfortingly, "pretend we're at the fried chicken spot."

"Okay," Giselle managed, taking a couple of deep breaths. "It's just a restaurant."

"It's just a restaurant," Rose repeated, combing through the entrees while quietly calculating cost in his mind. "Whatever you decide just please don't pick the filet mignon."

Giselle squinted up at Rose and then back down at the menu. She scanned to see if the item had a description next to it but she decided to wing it.

"Oh no, don't worry about that; I don't eat fish," Giselle appeased comically.

"What? You're kidding, right?" asked Rose, seeking clarification.

"No, I'm serious. I think I'm allergic. The last time I ate it I broke out in all these bumps—"

"No, it's not that. Filet mignon isn't fish, it's beef," Rose elucidated.

"Oops. It's not like filet-o-fish?" Giselle asked, on the threshold of embarrassment.

"This isn't McDonald's. I mean I know I said to pretend we're back in the hood, but come on, girl."

"I'm sorry," Giselle said giggling. "I figured because it had the word 'filet' in it. Never mind. Brain fart. Putrid smelling brain fart and now we should both move on from it."

Rose attempted to aid her. "Look here, it says 'salmon steak.' Is it salmon or is it a steak? This place is confusing. And I don't see any prices either. Does this mean it's free or does it mean we'll be washing dishes? I need to know so I can go to the bank and take out a loan."

Rose's efforts at making Giselle feel better were not lost on her. She caressed his hand, indicating that she would like to weigh in, which was a departure from her usual gall. Rose silenced.

"Is there anything here that you haven't had before?" the double entendre lettuce-wrapped around an innocent delivery.

"Yeah, the garganelli pasta with duck. I've never eaten that in my life," Rose told, still skimming the menu. "And you?" he returned blindly, walking right into the obvious trap.

"Well, I haven't had you yet," Giselle suggested sensually, as Rose quickly pulled his hand back to avoid the delicate contact of their warming skin.

"The reason we're here: Ash Wednesday massacre," Rose reminded, turning the conversation back to the business section.

"Do we have to talk about this now? Let's enjoy the ambiance," Giselle said with a chuckle. Rose managed a nervous laugh of his own and began to examine the wine list. Giselle twirled her fork as the perceptible New York City mystique floated in the air like a veritable Thanksgiving Day parade balloon.

"What do you drink, Giselle?"

"Like, drink drink?"

"Yes, like *drink* drink."

"Well, when I used to chill with my *niggas* I drank Hennessy or Cobra beer. But when I would go clubbing I'd drink Alize or 'thug passion'."

Rose scanned around to see if anyone had heard Giselle.

"Thug passion? Do you really think they'll have 'thug passion' at Tavern on the Green?"

"Redbull and vodka?" Giselle shot back enthusiastically.

"I don't think so. How about we go with some *vino*. Let's do wine instead."

"I got you. Keepin' it classy, right?"

Giselle awkwardly winked at Rose. Her poise was coming slightly unraveled under the lens of the sophisticated setting. Underneath the table, Giselle rubbed her foot against the inside of Rose's leg just as a waiter approached. Rose jumped in his seat, bumping his knee against the bottom of the table. He caught the glassware just before it fell and settled the rattling silverware.

"Good save—hi, my name is Shawn. I'll be your server tonight. What can I start you off with?"

Giselle held her laughter as Rose reprimanded her with his eyes. He arranged his words in his mind before replying, as the waiter processed the apparent age difference.

"So she'll have the filet mignon and a glass of merlot and I'll go with the roast duck and a glass of Riesling," Rose surprisingly requested. He side-glanced at Giselle who was feeding him approval.

"Excellent choices," returned the waiter. "No appetizers for the lovely couple?"

"Buffalo wings?" chimed Giselle, wielding her winning charm advantageously.

"No buffalo wings tonight," declared Rose, almost as an edict. "But bring over a bottle of thug passion if you have any in the back."

The waiter's face wrinkled up as if he had smelled something rancid. He drifted away from the eaters and then they began to visually nibble on each other. Rose took in Giselle's crystal chandelier earrings. Giselle noticed the length of his eyelashes; they were long for a male. The dancing flame from the table's lone candle cast an ethereal glow upon Giselle's face, which was even more impassioned than usual tonight. Rose noticed it but fought hard not to get captured by it.

"So, are we going back to your place after this or a hotel or . . .?"

"Look, Giselle, there's a line—"

"Which you've already crossed, I'd say."

"No I haven't," Rose said as if trying to convince every patron in the restaurant. "This is just dinner. I'm here for information."

Giselle leaned forward causing Rose's eyes to plunge down her plummeting neckline.

"You're here for dessert," Giselle stated, offering herself up as if an imaginary, fruited, sugar-sprinkled dish.

A mysterious, muscular man, seated at a nearby table with a female companion, had started to take notice of Rose and the peculiar happenings. Rose felt the heat of the man's eyes examining him and began perspiring from his hairline. He paled in color and then reached for the blush napkin which blanketed his utensils. At that precise moment, the waiter returned, placing down the palatable platters.

"*Bon appetit.*"

Giselle stared at her plate, intimidated by it.

"Oh, it has a flower on it. Are you sure this is edible?"

Rose removed the flower from her plate and gingerly placed it in the front section of Giselle's hair. She gave a girly giggle and adjusted it in place. She resumed sizing up her dish.

"That's like . . . art. I don't know if I'm supposed to eat this, frame it, or—"

"Eat it, regurgitate it, then frame it," interrupted Rose. "It could pass for a Jackson Pollock, his later stuff, of course."

"That's gross. Who's Jackson Pollock?"

"He's nobody tonight," said Rose, his attention now divided.

"Is that because there's only you and me tonight?" she nudged.

"It's you and *I*," Rose corrected. Not instantly realizing the encouragement Giselle received from this. He didn't intend to agree with her, but he didn't really intend to do anything that he had done to this point.

"The moon looks so weightless tonight. A huge, majestic medallion on the necklace that is the sky."

"That's a fancy analogy, Giselle. You know. . . I love the moon—"

"I love *you*."

Rose practically spat out an entire mouthful of Riesling. Giselle had timed it perfectly. He dabbed frantically with a napkin at his mouth as Giselle basked in the advantage that she appeared to have as his restaurant etiquette, and his cool, melted away under the fluster of her revelation. She leaned back like an arsonist admiring her blaze, trying to prolong that incendiary moment.

"Okay, Giselle. Ash Wednesday," Rose pivoted. "Three guys killed. They had families, you know."

"Fuck them. They were drug dealing scum. They got wacked over turf!"

"Keep it down," Rose hushed. "What about the old lady, huh? That was somebody's grandmother."

"Look. I'll tell you who did it. I will. You'll know before tonight is over. I promise. Just not now."

"Fine," Rose relinquished. "Eat your food then."

"Feed it to me."

"Oh hell no," Rose returned, refusing verbally and physically with his hand animations.

Giselle threw her napkin down, feigning as if she was leaving. Rose begrudgingly cut the tender meat which had already cooled on Giselle's plate. He looked around and felt the burn of the mystery man's eyes penetrating his exposed flesh. He nevertheless placed the food in Giselle's mouth, leveraging the fork out by wedging the meat against Giselle's bottom teeth and pulling. Giselle chewed sensually, as if she was chewing up Rose himself.

"This is really good *meat*. Which isn't fish or chicken," she said, washing down the steak with a mouthful of merlot. Rose swirled in his chair as if he was swirling around in her glass. He was swimming in it, trying to find the shallow end of the tilt so he could breathe. She had grown to the size of a whale now and he fought to not go into her throat. But his consumption was a virtual inevitability.

"Easy with the wine," he warned, attempting to exercise his slipping authority. "That's not iced tea."

"You're the one giving alcohol to a minor, you bad, bad boy, you," she dramatized.

"Oh, *shi-i-it!*" Rose released, elongating the word as if it were polysyllabic. "Damn. It's just that you look and act so much older that I forget you're just a . . ."

"Kid?" Giselle completed. "A little girl? Isn't that what you called me the day we first met? Well, I'm not a little girl anymore. I'm almost seventeen. I'm a woman."

"You're a woman," Rose replied, somewhere in between a statement and a question. Rose snuck a glance at the voyeur couple observing from their table and then back at his dance partner for the night. He flung his napkin angrily.

"I know this fucking asshole is internal affairs," he grumbled.

"What guy, who are you talking about? The corny ass waiter?"

"No, not the waiter!"

"Can we dance after dessert?" Giselle asked, strategically changing the subject. "And I mean real dessert, not *me* dessert. I mean . . . if that isn't crossing the line."

"Maybe—I could use the fresh air," Rose conceded.

"That's exactly what I was thinking," Giselle agreed, as destiny and momentum began leading them in the direction of the moonlit courtyard and their predestined stage marks.

The waiter returned with two more glasses as Rose and Giselle simultaneously finished off their previous. Rose cut another piece of filet mignon for Giselle. She sucked it in and held the fork for an extra second in between her protruding, lustful lips. She licked the juice from the steak off her lips as her mouth reddened from the wine she was slurping from out of her elegant merlot glass.

"Dammit, this wine's gone right through me. Excuse me, I'm gonna go . . . um . . . drain the lizard," Rose clumsily disclosed.

"You have a lizard?" she teased.

Rose stumbled from his seat and zigzagged between tables toward the bathroom door where he and the enigmatic man converged.

"Age before beauty," stated the ghost and Rose hesitantly entered first.

Once tensely at the urinal, Rose felt the man uncomfortably close to him as he relieved himself. The man pulled a black gun, inside a holster, from out of his pants and placed it atop the urinal. Rose panicked and felt for his own gun, trying not to pee on his hand now. The food that he had just picked at came back up a little, filling the sides of his cheeks with an unpleasant alkaline taste. Another bead formed on his forehead.

"That's a hot piece of ass you got with you tonight. Is that your girl or just something you're—"

"Oh no," Rose refuted, not giving him the opportunity to actually pronounce the vulgar verb. "I'm not . . . *hitting* that, if that's what you're thinking. That's my . . ."

"That's your bitch and that's all right," he said crassly.

"No. That's not my girl," Rose protested. "We're not a couple. I'm just here to get some information from her for my career, that's all. This is job related."

"Okay. Relax, guy. You know you *can* get ass. Especially a piece like that. I was actually just going to congratulate you."

"Congratulate me? Yeah, sure. No thank you." Rose zipped up and zipped out. "Enjoy your evening with your wife, sir," he released in the air behind him.

That's not my wife either," the man said, busting out in loud, cacophonous laughter. Rose brushed past the sink without washing his hands, pushed through the door and rushed back to his seat. He fell back into his chair, almost taking the table cloth and the place settings with him.

"Everything come out all right?" she asked sarcastically.

Rose could feel droplets of urine on his underwear but he softly nodded and searched for the server book on the table.

"It's done. All taken care of," Giselle nonchalantly informed.

"Are you serious?"

"No, I'm Giselle. And I know how much you make. I know how hard you work. No one's ever taken me to a place like this. And this is my way of saying thank you."

"How did you pay for this?"

"Cash."

"No shit, cash," Rose said indignantly. "But how?"

And it was then that Rose realized that dirty money paid for his meal. He brushed over the serial number of his bank card as if reading brail. He flicked at it with his middle finger, feeling sullied by her gesture. Giselle pointed to the courtyard—stood up tall—and slinkily extended her hand; her exhibitionism collecting eyes and revising conversations. And a boozy Giselle walked a conflicted Rose into the courtyard, her dainty hand pulling his sweaty one. Romantic music entered the courtyard as if cinematically as the two awkwardly locked fingers. It felt like the prom that Giselle would never have and she stole the homecoming queen crown, shining brightly under the resplendent moonlight which lit them like actors. The elegant pair began to gradually move in sync. Giselle pressed herself up against Rose's stiff body, bringing her lips to his face. Rose pulled away, rejecting her ostensible affection.

"Relax, weirdo. I'm not trying to kiss you."

"I mean, with you, I have to be prepared for anything," Rose shot back.

"Well, I hope you're prepared for *this*: Diablo and Kilo shot all those people on Ash Wednesday," she unexpectedly began. "They are considered to be the lieutenants in the drug cartel. They serve the *Capos* from Honduras. Diablo blasted the old lady because she was dialing 911, that wasn't planned, but it shows just how evil they are. They rent an apartment at 711 Fairplace—5D. They rarely go out during the night, so you never see them. I'll tell you when they make their next gun deal. How many pieces they're moving and where they're carrying them. Then . . . your detective hopes . . . your *police dreams* can finally come true."

Giselle practically held Rose up as this information threatened to floor him.

"'Diablo' and 'Kilo'? Those are their names?" Rose verified. "And they live in 5D? That's the top floor, far right apartment, right?"

"Far *left*. I can get you the guns they used, so you can get a search warrant for all the other guns. You can bust them, dead to rights. And they'll be done."

Rose, having just received the information he so desperately sought, momentarily forgot that Giselle was in his arms. She brought her body closer to him and reminded him. He held her tighter now, a sense of ownership over her body suddenly influencing their embrace. They clutched each other, but both exhibited awkwardness. Rose stalled via conversation.

"You know, I never asked you what you wanted to be, right? Did I?"

"I want to be a writer," she stated with ardor.

"Really? Giselle the writer, huh? That's nice. Do you write poetry or short stories or . . .?"

"I write all types of things. But right now I'm working on a love story."

"A love story?" Rose repeated.

"A love story," Giselle affirmed. "But there's something else that I'd also like to be too."

"And what is that?" he requested, fearing the ensuing.

"The words on your lips. The source of your bliss. The taste on your kiss. That's a poem. And so is this."

Giselle assertively grabbed Rose's face and stood on the tips of her toes to kiss him. She practically came out of her heels as the poetry of the positioning of their bodies organically manifested. Rose pulled away, a strange ballet in which he pulled his neck farther as he pulled her body closer. She palmed the back of his head—practically forcing him to kiss her—and opened her warm, moist mouth.

"We can't do this, this is wrong," he offered meekly.

"I just gave you the information you needed. I'm risking my life for you. I changed the way I live for *you*," Giselle told, heat and hunger emanating from her aroused body.

"How do I justify this?" he asked, as if begging God at that precise moment.

Rose tried to resist but it was impossible at this point. The lullaby was tender and sweet and was drowsing them into indivisible communion. The alcohol was doing its job, impairing them as they coalesced and swayed in the breeze of their moment. The splendor of the New York City venue and the magnitude of the night were working against Rose's urge to resist like a relentless riptide. And then there was her spell, it was extra strong tonight—as if she had sprayed it on from an antique perfume bottle and then particleized into the air herself. She entered Rose from various ports of entry like a vapor. Rose's defenses collapsed brick by brick and then, it appeared to me, that their lips acquainted. They slipped into the shadows, for forbidden intimacy, Giselle caressing the back of Rose's head and disheveling his thick, product-filled hair. His hands carefully glided down her back—almost to the curvature of her butt. Their faces were hidden from view, but surely they were not simply conversing anymore. Rose lifted her up but her elegant shoes remained planted in the gravel. Her toes, stuck to her transparent black stockings by her scarlet toenail polish, curled and then a lamp's light lent illumination to the reciprocal assault. A cut on Rose's lip had reopened and a tiny trickle of blood rested on the swollen, raised ridge of his lower lip. Giselle sucked it away from Rose, savoring its metallic taste. She further invaded his mouth with her tongue, sucking out white wine essences that he had apparently been savoring. She stole that and every word that could possibly come out of his mouth to gloss the prohibited proceedings there.

The two just gazed at each other: lipstick smeared, a speck of blood reemerging on Rose's mouth, their hair a mess. Rose dabbed at his bottom lip with his sleeve. Giselle stared at him like a life-sized porcelain mannequin staring at customers through a freshly Windexed store window. The two simply stood in the aftermath of that pivotal moment, just them and the cooling night now, everything encased in a globe. They had journeyed into each other, losing control in a moment they could not un-live. She had finally reached the ventricle of his heart, traveling far deeper than they had ever thought possible. He looked for a place to hide, to disappear into, settling in on one particular cloud-like sliver of her eye, which was as large as the eye in Magritte's *The False Mirror*. He remained there, but once she blinked the wind created by her claw-like eyelashes would drag him inward, into her optic nerve and he'd likely fall all the way into her heart, where it appeared he was anticipated anyway.

They held each other and pushed each other away simultaneously, achieving and erasing nothing, excluding messy enmeshment. It was like trying to undo the silk of a spider's web from both sides—while the spider clung to the opposing threads—without allowing the spider to fall. The spider would simply *have* to fall. And perhaps *they* simply fell on this night. Perhaps it was hyperbole. But they were certainly descending, wondering how the hell they smashed into each other after previously orbiting one another like satellites. Rose blanketed Giselle in his dinner jacket, asking God how he would reverse the catastrophic damage he had just caused. It was an empty prayer. She listened to his heartbeat and fell asleep standing up as the curtain fell silently on their roaring night of passion without either tainted player taking a bow.

Chapter VIII

Having returned home, Rose furiously foamed his head with shampoo, attempting to clear it. He scrubbed at suds as if he was trying to get rid of lice and memory as his eyes reddened and sunk from sadness. Rose lathered up his lean, muscular body; he scoured hard and fast at mild grime from perspiring and extreme guilt. Outside his apartment door, keys jingled unmusically. A lock turned, followed by a short pause, and then a second lock turning obtusely. The sound of streaming water prevented Rose from hearing any of this, even when the door creaked open loudly and a familiar personage entered the foyer. She tiptoed clandestinely through the living room before her knee collided violently with a coffee table, flattening frames holding Rose and Cecelia's cherished memories. Rose heard this and reached for his gun, still situated in the holster clipped to the belt on his pants, which were wrapped around the toilet seat. In the living room, a silhouette interrupted the predictable shadows of the apartment, her hand fumbling for a light switch, flicking at where it might be.

"Stop or I'll fucking shoot!" commanded Rose, suppressing the trigger ever so slightly.

"It's me! It's me! It's me!" she answered, terror altering the pitch of her voice. "It's Cecelia!"

When the lights came on, they revealed a soap-covered Rose, with his service weapon punched out in front of him, zeroing in on the center mass of his fiancée. Perhaps only her unforgettable eyes prevented him from shooting her, as she was wrapped in a plaid scarf and adorned with a stylish, red beret.

"What in the hell are you doing here?" he griped breathlessly, lowering the muzzle.

"Well, that's not the reaction I was expecting," she complained.

"I wasn't expecting *you*. Why didn't you call first?"

94

"Call? I was trying to surprise you!"

"Well, shit, you surprised me all right. Surprised the living shit outta' me! I thought it was a burglar or something."

"Burglars have keys now? And when are you going to freaking hug me? I've only been standing here for a minute already."

Rose dropped his guard finally and wrapped his body around Cecelia.

"If you ever point a gun at me again, I'll kill you," she said, combing back Rose's wet hair with her wavering hands.

She held on to his naked body, massaging him in the process. The pair finally kissed after thousands of miles, missed milestones, and stolen memories. Cecelia noticed the cut on Rose's lip and attempted to soothe it. Rose removed her fingers from his mouth, downplaying the minor nick. What had truly been punctured was their bond. Rose lifted Cecelia up, closer to his torso and repeated the words "I'm sorry" numerous times. Cecelia draped herself around him, her clothes absorbing the water off his flesh. Rose put her down after some time, and searched for clothes to hide his shamed body. He hastily folded the suit jacket he wore earlier and side-kicked his patent leather shoes into the dust den underneath his bed. He sought to change the tenor of the night by selecting a bottle of red wine that he could consume with the woman to whom he was still engaged. Cecelia playfully snatched the pinot noir from his clutches.

"Enjoy with friends. Pairs well with beef, steak, or filet mignon," she recited off the back label.

Rose, paradoxically, laughed at her proper pronunciation of the dish. He recalled the filet mignon malapropism with Giselle and remorse filtered in.

"So, how's the job going?" Cecelia asked, hoping to reacquaint immediately.

"I don't really want to talk about that right now," returned Rose, knowing that any conversation related to the job could inextricably lead them to Giselle.

"I'm curious, baby," Cecelia insisted, her voice sweetly softening. "I want to know what it is you do. What's going on in the streets. Any good collars lately? Any—what's it called—*eighty-fives* lately?"

Rose flared slightly at Cecelia's questioning. They both acknowledged tension in their facial expressions, and Rose's frustration was even more palpable.

"If you really want to know what's going on here, you shouldn't have left. I could be telling you all about it every day when I walk through that door. But you decided to go study as far away from me as humanly possible without actually leaving the country, so maybe you don't deserve to know."

The harshness of Rose's words pierced Cecelia's countenance. He noticed this and yet he continued on with resentment in his voice.

"I chase mopes around all day. I get bullshit weed collars when I'm trying to get gun collars. My *G.I. Joe* lieutenant and *dyke* sergeant can't stand each other—so that provides some entertaining drama at roll calls. Oh, and on the subject of drama," Rose continued, riding the momentum of his emotions, "I now have to protect a sixteen-year-old witness because she tipped me off to these murders on Ash Wednesday. Would you like me to go on?"

"Lose the attitude," Cecelia reprimanded, gathering up her own anger now to channel at Rose. "I just sat on a plane for six hours to see you. And first you point a gun at me and then you go on this dickhead rant?"

"I'm sorry . . ."

"You're damn right, you're sorry!"

"*Ce-ce*, I apologize. I am very happy to see you, it's just that . . ." Rose struggled to find the words. He pictured Cecelia and Giselle concurrently all in the same reflection and tried to somehow explain away his actions in a way that made sense in the aggregate.

"I strap a gun to my side. I Velcro up a bullet proof vest and I patrol the worst goddamn neighborhoods in the Bronx. The people in there despise us and they'd shoot me in the face if I gave them the opportunity. The future isn't promised. *Tomorrow* isn't even promised. You're out there taking pictures while we could be here in New York City actually living life and having real things to photograph."

Illusory images of the Empire State Building, Tavern on the Green, a snow-covered gazebo in the heart of Central Park and the prancing water fountains of the Columbus Circle roundabout filled Rose's quixotic mind.

"I don't need to hear this right now. How is your mom doing?" Cecelia asked, bringing the dreamer back to reality.

"My mom is fine—I miss her like crazy. She's in Florida cleaning up my aunt's shit. No mother and no fiancée. I literally have no women in my life."

"What? Why would you say that?" inquired Cecelia, suspicion breeding at the bottom of her question.

"Say wh—?"

"That you have no women in your life?" she interrupted. "Why would you tell me that?"

"Well, I rarely hear from my mom. She's got her hands full taking care of her sister, who has Alzheimer's, you might recall. And you're away on the west coast doing your photography scholarship so I . . ."

"True, but my family is in Puerto Rico; you're here in New York. I'm all alone too. You don't see me losing my mind. I don't need anyone."

"And I need someone?"

"I don't know, maybe you do. You just said it funny, that's all I'm prepared to say right now."

Cecelia began snooping around the room before Rose intercepted her. She sidestepped him and continued surveying the apartment before Rose cut her off again. He gently, tenderly kissed Cecelia, a small match going off between them. He looked deeply into her melancholy eyes, trying to say something with a look. Her eyes begged for truthfulness at this point.

"I love you," he said, almost out of habit.

"That's not what I need to hear from you right now," she submitted, disappointedly.

Familiarity began to effectively thaw that iceberg which stood between them. Rose guided her in the direction of an old reliable couch and they both fell onto it, dust *poofing* up and cushions flattening underneath their tumbling bodies. Toes met heels as shoes were removed and impishly kicked into the air. Zippers were unzipped and buttons detached from buttonholes. Her feminine flesh fell out from fabric and it soon turned uninhibitedly sensual. Rose loved his woman without the limitations of his mores impeding his amatory motions. To end the night, and after so many lonely nights . . .

Love was made.

In Rose's room, a young lady rested on his heart, listening to its music, tracking the beats as they distinguished themselves from the other sounds in the apartment. Her silhouette was clean, her dark brown hair particularly placable. It could have been Giselle lying on him, but it's likelier that it was Cecelia. Rose caressed the girl as if she was a newborn baby. They drowsed into an intertwined sleep, with their fingers interlocked but perhaps not quite in perfect emotional harmony.

The following day, Cecelia and Rose joined hands in Central Park as they rediscovered precious gems of New York City. Rose twirled her under a rustic gazebo, taking in the moments of their shared time together through the excited eyes of young children. Once they stopped spinning, they etched their initials in the weathered wooden baluster for all time. They traveled down to Bowery Street to visit an old bespectacled Jewish jeweler there and have her engagement ring re-polished under steam—as they admired wedding bands. In the evening, they jogged through a worn out trail in Riverdale before returning downtown on the music-carrying number one train. They joined the zigging line at their favorite movie theater, just a stone's throw from Lincoln Center, where many of their pennies had gone into the plaza's water fountain, wishing for a lifetime of moments like these. The two fed each other popcorn and gummi bears while watching a World War Two drama engrossed in their cozy, reclined seats. When they returned home, they once again slept, limbs over limbs, linked by a longstanding love.

Five days elapsed like a wedding reception slideshow. Cecelia and Rose embraced and parted sorrowfully at John F. Kennedy airport. They held on to each other, hoping life would somehow change its unbending mind and keep them together on the same coast. She was off to the Golden City and he had business to finish up in grimy Gotham. Jet engines roared, their hearts roared—yelling to be close to each other. But reality parted them again and distance and time would soon get back to work at sabotaging their love.

When Rose returned back to the dingy fifty-first precinct, he and his fellow rookies trudged into the muster room lethargic and lacking inspiration. They assembled like balls on a billiard table after being struck by the cue ball; they all sort of rolled into no particular spot or order.

"Line it up!" yelled Lieutenant Garret, frightening the cops into formation. "Get the lead out of your asses and give me four neat ranks. Matter-a' fact, make it look perfect. Lieutenant Angulo from Bronx Internal Affairs is here to address you. I don't know who fucked up, but the last thing I need is the rat squad shoving a microscope up my ass."

The recruits guided off each other and ultimately resembled a respectable platoon. Lieutenant Angulo entered, looking completely unvarnished in his stark white NYPD lieutenant's blouse. When Rose viewed his face, he was certain that this was the man who had conversed with him at the urinal at Tavern on the Green. Rose had the urge to run to the bathroom again, but instead he pulled the brim of his eight-point hat down over his eyes to conceal any features that might identify him to the high ranker.

"A week and a half ago," began the lieutenant, "some officers from this precinct allowed two suspects to walk away following a vicious beating up on the strip."

He began scanning the nervous rookies for any tells of transgressions.

"Witnesses say those guys identified themselves as cops and were given a free pass. We do not tolerate the shit-canning of IAB jobs! You get to the scene and the perp is a cop, you throw your cuffs on him, secure his firearm, and call for a supervisor."

Rose swallowed hard. He felt his career unravelling, the ball of yarn becoming smaller and smaller with each word that projected from the imposing boss's chapped lips.

"It's not up to you to give some degenerate cop a 'get out of jail free' card. The victim from that night's screw-up is now deaf in one ear and every lawyer in New York wants to represent him. It's become a *magila*, and I'm left holding the bag of shit. I do not like bags of shit. They're unpleasant. So I'm leaving my card in case anyone has the balls to come forward. Don't make me open up Pandora's box, because believe me it won't be pretty. We had cake and we had cock and we're all out of cake. What does that leave?"

The recruits stared blankly while the white shirt waited for an answer that never came.

"Exactly. A big, black, veiny one."

Rose anticipated Angulo calling his name or recognizing him from their recent restaurant collision. Surely he couldn't dodge two bullets simultaneously. But Angulo walked out of the room, and Rose took a colossal breath and contemplated how he would avoid falling off a cliff that was quickly crumbling underneath the shit ingrained grooves of his heavying work boots.

No sooner did Rose arrive on post that night than Giselle caprioled into his arms with the enthusiasm of a lotto winner. Yes, there is indeed a way that you go into someone's arm when you're theirs. She went in twice as confident. Rose caught her because that's what was expected of him.

"Where the hell have you been?" she scolded more so than asked.

"Vacation," he answered, free of any emotion.

"So, we finally have our moment, our *forever* moment and you just vanish without telling me?"

Rose paused and considered his response, realizing he was skating on a barely frozen lake.

"You had a forever moment with this broad?" Cheddar chastised, holding Rose hostage for the due response.

"We didn't have a *forever* . . . can you please go over there. Please. For a minute. Go there," Rose directed, pointing to a spot in the distance as Cheddar pantomimed the universal "I'm watching you" gesture at his partner.

"You're ashamed of what happened, aren't you?" Giselle semi-whispered, her eyes big and her body small as a mouse and looking meek against the large backdrop of the night.

"What happened? Tell me. In your eyes, what occurred that night?"

"Well . . ." Giselle organized her thoughts in her blown mind like index cards. "We . . . I . . . I gave you my heart. I mean, I gave you information, that you wanted for a long, long time, right? So . . . I'm going to get you what you need for a search warrant, like we agreed and . . ."

It hurt Rose to see Giselle struggle to piece together a sentence that was acceptable and made sense under the convoluted circumstances.

"So we are talking about the same thing?" Rose asked, trying to sort out the metaphysics of the situation.

"Of course we are," Giselle replied maturely.

"Look, whatever you do, from here on out, you have to be careful. You do not need to take any unnecessary risks. I got this," Rose said reassuringly, perhaps not fully believing that he actually had *it*.

"Of course. My seventeenth birthday is on Saturday," Giselle reminded with jazz in her voice. "Museum of Natural History? I'd also like to go to Central Park and take a picture at the gazebo."

"Gazebo," Rose repeated numbly. "So you actually made it to seventeen, huh? That's an accomplishment here. Congratulations, Giselle. Happy Birth—"

"Saturday. Say it to me on Saturday, we'll carve our names in the gazebo to commemorate the big day. So bring your pocketknife."

Giselle was typically insistent. Rose pictured that octagon gazebo which now stood as a duplicate symbol of his deepening dilemma. Rose took her in, once again getting tangled up in the length of her mascaraed eyelashes, which at the moment seemed longer than the actual length of time that they had known each other. He pointed to her untied laces. Before she could bend down to tie them, he went to a knee and tied a perfect knot for her. Giselle reached over Rose's shoulder, her cold belt buckle making contact with his forehead, and pulled his memo book out from his rear right pocket. Their positioning gave the impression of inappropriateness. Giselle autographed his book and wrote "Officer on post, no violations observed." She scanned the page, extending the moment to take in Rose's feminine handwriting. She read that the color of the day was orange, like the sky, although it had already begun to turn pink. Her ambitions were also ripening on an evening that was young but would carry drama deep into its twilight. She took note of the return date before handing Rose back his memorandum pad; he was already standing up and waiting for it. He smiled at her exaggerated signature, the "i" in her name dotted with a tiny heart. Cheddar interrupted the love fest.

"Was that a forever moment or an infinity second or . . .?"

"That was a never mind moment," Rose responded.

He would not get to hug Giselle; it would have been too awkward. He longed to though. He yearned to do and say so much in that moment. He imagined himself plucking those pinkening clouds out of the sky, like cotton candy, swirling them around a paper cone of honored promises, restoring her faith in the goodness of man, and then shattering it by kissing the sugary residue off her light plum-colored lips. He wanted to rescue her from her manacles only to place her in a different type of entanglement: good intentioned, but nevertheless precarious and indecorous. She was a willing passenger for any voyage, so long as he was the vessel, and he knew this. Juggling this in his mind, he platonically patted her on her pretty head, brushed down her eyebrows with his thumb and withdrew toward his partner. Rose was lonely and faced the lonely night still. And light was quickly submitting to darkness and the compass that he concealed under his left breast pocket was largely misguiding him.

Giselle simply scootered off like she often did, but with far less pep. And he admired the motion of her body as he often did, but with far greater appreciation for her. In the charm bracelet of life, she was now somehow his favorite charm—the gold, good luck elephant with the diamond for an eye—making a bid to become the entire bracelet. She had finally gained the purchase on his heart that she had sought since the day she opened her eyes to him. It was unclear if she would get to enjoy this favorable position. Rose and Cheddar eventually strolled off and he ultimately stopped into a pharmacy and hand-picked a birthday card for his young acquaintance. Cheddar ridiculed him for that as well, beating him down for the duration of the night over it.

"Let me write in her card too," he would ask periodically.

The two continued to amble against the night and soon arrived at an imposing cathedral-like church. Palm fronds were strewn on the ground like Monday morning litter, so Rose folded them up into the shape of a cross, pressing his creation against his heart.

"You ever notice how our precinct has so many churches and temples in it?" Rose inquired.

"Yeah, it's a waste of space in my opinion. I mean, given the neighborhood, wouldn't you say?"

"No," Rose disagreed. "People are in there. They believe. There's still faith here."

"How can a place with so much faith have so little hope?" Cheddar raised, mixing God and fatalism in a grave question whose answer Rose had been preparing thoughtfully in his mind.

"Hope is still present here. I've seen it in instances. You see it in the good deeds that certain people do. These people aren't doomed yet. I haven't seen any signs reading "abandon hope all ye who enter here." God has not abandoned this place altogether," Rose declared with a certain assuredness that belied the celestial uncertainty of all matters godly and heavenly.

"Oh yeah? When did you become the Pope?" Cheddar asked mockingly. "Dear Lord, help me shoot a cop tonight: the daily prayer here. God left this shithole a long time ago."

"That's not true," debated Rose. "God is here. You just have to look a little harder to find him. That's the beauty of God sometimes. If he was so easy to see, everybody would believe. And that's the true test."

"God is gone. It's the Devil's town. His soldiers work here, and they haven't exactly started a fan club for us. What I'm trying to say is . . . they fucking hate us."

"They don't hate *us*," Rose contested, "they're unhappy with their life in the slum—with the poverty. They languish in destitute conditions and then the city sends us in to try and resolve all their problems for them. Maybe they hate themselves or the uniforms on our backs. But if you take off that NYPD blue, they're probably giving you a *pound* on the corner when you pass them. But as long as we keep working for the 'racist' police department, an agency in the 'oppressive' government, they'll keep wiping their asses with our City of New York paycheck."

"Wipe their asses with it? They should thank me every two weeks for the free shit they get from my paycheck. And they better keep my paycheck free from shit so the cashier can read it and they can get the money on to their Benefit Card to buy toilet paper so they won't have to use my paycheck to wipe their filthy asses in the first place," Cheddar complexly quipped, celebrating what he believed to be cleverness.

"Well played, my friend, but you should get direct deposit," Rose returned, before flipping at the brim of Cheddar's eight-point hat and knocking it off his head. Cheddar assumed a boxing stance and threw two soft jabs at Rose's moving head, and the partners play-fought their way to post as co-conspirators to a blooming friendship.

Back at the precinct, phones rang rudely, interrupting typing, report writing, fighting—between caged prisoners and the cops processing their paperwork—as the normal bustle of precinct life hustled along.

"Five-one precinct, Officer Smith speaking."

First there was a lengthy pause, then a familiar voice shone through rather lucidly.

"Yes, good evening. My name is Officer Matos, from the *four-eight* and I borrowed a flashlight from an Officer Rose at your precinct. I'm trying to get in touch with him so I can return it to him."

"And how do I know you're actually a cop?" interrogated Smith.

"That is a very fair question," Giselle responded. "The color of the day for plain clothes today is orange. And the return date for c summonses is July 27th."

These two pieces of privileged information were enough for Smith to release Rose's cell phone number to his aggressive admirer.

"Six-four-six . . . four-eight-seven . . ."

At 711 Fairplace Avenue, Giselle placed two black pistols—the instruments of death from the Ash Wednesday murders—into her backpack. At the entrance to the building, four males from a separate cartel, armed heavily with concealed firearms, approached exuding menacing auras. It was just a few short blocks from there that Rose mundanely wrote a parking ticket to a vehicle that was one in a row of numerous double parked cars.

"*Yo'* Cheddar, what's today's date? I think I can make my whole month on this block."

"Remember, we don't have quotas anymore, we have *performance objectives.* You can let one or two go," Cheddar teased. "And today is April first my friend . . . Oh shit, Palm Sunday and April Fools' Day fell on the same day this year. That's a cruel joke."

"Well . . . April *is* the cruelest month breeding Lilacs out of the dead land, mixing memory and desire," Rose recited drearily, recalling "The Wasteland," one of his most frequently read poems.

At that precise moment Rose's cell phone began to vibrate inside of a small pocket of his bulletproof vest, interrupting the monotonous with the scandalous. He lazily brought his phone to his ear.

"They're about to deal guns on the roof of 711 Fairplace, right now!" Giselle informed breathlessly.

"Giselle? Hello, is this Giselle? How in the hell did you get my number?"

"Forget about that, they have crazy guns up there! Just bring plenty of backup!" she advised hysterically. "I gotta go . . . I love you, Brandon."

Giselle concluded the phone call and looked over her petite, sylph-like shoulder, and viewed her very imperilment in the figure of the heartless Diablo hovering over her. The maddened crime boss snatched up Giselle with both hands as she produced not a single sound of protest.

As Rose and Cheddar sprinted into the courtyard in front of the doomed drug den, Giselle's compact body was situated above the wind, which pushed her hair and the fabric of her modish ensemble skyward into the low floating clouds. For a moment, she eclipsed the moon and cast temporary darkness over Fairplace. The young girl involuntarily fluttered as her body roared toward earth, until its fall was fatally interrupted by the unforgiving concrete just in front of Rose and Cheddar's scuffed boots. A nauseating *splat* sound reverberated in between the graffiti-garnished tryptic, pushing a tidal wave of blood onto Rose's uniform, hands, and face.

Rose took in Giselle's fallen body and collapsed directly onto her, shielding her shattered skeleton from the view of anyone else. His palm cross fell toward the ground as if hell-bound. It spun supernaturally, like a flaming Ferris wheel, and hit with the force of a bomb dropped from a plane. In a moment, Giselle and Rose and his holy palm and the sky had cataclysmically fallen—all in the same courtyard.

"God!" Rose manically yelled, through a cracking voice. Cheddar unholstered his weapon and pointed it at the roof from which Giselle was heaved. He yanked at Rose's jacket, trying to lift him up.

"Brandon, get up! Brandon, get up partner, we aren't safe here!"

Rose attempted to resuscitate Giselle. He received a mouthful of blood which she gurgled up from her throat and he caught on his tongue. Rose angrily spat out Giselle's blood, which now dripped from his quivering lips.

"Central, I need an *eighty-five* forthwith!" Cheddar demanded into his radio. "I got a female down and she's *likely*, Central! The perps are still on the scene, send me everybody you got!"

The dispatcher transmitted three consecutive beeps, signifying an emergency. Patrol vehicles surged illuminatingly toward the location of the fallen. Once again, police sirens became the soundtrack of the night. Rose breathed all the air from his lungs into Giselle, desperately pumping her chest. Finally, an ambulance arrived as a huge, rowdy crowd began to incite. EMS personnel had to shove Rose off of Giselle, and he wore the burgundy of Giselle's blood on his face like a sacramental mask. Lieutenant Garret arrived in his unmarked Impala, pushing the spectators back with his baton.

"Everybody back up. Back the *fuck* up!" he ordered, lawfully.

Garret attempted to lift Rose's body off the ground, but it was like trying to raise an anchor. He picked Rose halfway up, and then both men stumbled backward and fell hard onto the uncompromising terrain. Rose's bloodstained face startled the lieutenant, and Giselle's fluid trickled onto the lieutenant's stark white dress shirt. A deep, angry auburn was slowly absorbed by pristine white cotton. Rose climbed over Garret and grabbed Giselle's face for the last time. He held it, before gently closing her eyes with his thumbs and brushing strands of hair away from her face, just like in their initial meeting. She bled badly and he himself was bleeding with remorse, regret, and rage. The lieutenant ordered Rose to compose himself, but it was as if life had cut off one of his limbs and expected him to just carry on living. Rose crumpled into his own chest cavity—arms out—like he was simultaneously being crucified and, perhaps, surrendering. Giselle's body was *zapped* by electricity as EMS attempted to galvanize her back to life. Citizen's screamed at the sight of this, but the defibrillator continually shocked her and shoes inadvertently stomped on the sign of Christ's sacrifice. Boots trampled Rose's hand, crushing an extremity on his already crushed soul as he yelled in pain dually physical and emotional. And a bloodied, battered Rose reached for his symbolic palm and his sacrificial girl, both of which were now inhumanely buried under a chaotic pile of human limbs; the Shakespearean tragedy brought about by mutual overreaching and horrific human miscalculation.

CHAPTER IX

At the clandestine Internal Affairs Bronx site, a distraught Rose sat alone at a long wooden table as very little light entered the room. His bloodshot eyes stared downward, inexpressively, at the grooves of the table. His face was scuffed and his left hand was wrapped in bloodied bandages. Lieutenant Angulo, in a navy pinstriped suit, placed an ice cold glass of water next to Rose's elbow.

"Don't tip it over. And pick your head up. It goes like this: you play that 'blue wall of silence' bullshit with me and you'll be no different to me than any other Riker's Island inmate, except you won't have jelly to lube you up."

Rose slowly raised his head up and acclimated to his situation.

"I'm going to ask you some tough questions, and keep in mind that we already know the answers. We're asking them as a courtesy. Now, she called your phone five minutes before coming off that rooftop. What did she say to you? Go ahead, pal, save your pathetic career."

Rose tepidly sipped from the glass, the temperature of the water surprising him and hurting his teeth, awakening his senses in the process.

"Is this part of your tactics or you really don't recognize me?" Rose queried.

"Recognize you? Why in the hell would I recognize you?"

"Because you were following me. You followed me all the way into the bathroom of Tavern on the Green. You practically held my dick for me, with all due respect, Lieutenant."

"Speaking like that isn't going to help your cause, tough guy," warned the white shirt.

"What is my cause, huh? Why am I here?" begged Rose.

The lieutenant shook his head at Rose's moxie.

"You're here because you messed up. And you *know* that. The girl called your—wait, was that really you at the restaurant?" he glitched, bifurcating his thoughts while combing over Rose's features. "Holy shit, that *was* you! You were there with your little girlfriend the same day I was there with my wife, right? How about that?"

"Nice try, Lieutenant. But she wasn't my girlfriend. I don't think that was your wife either."

"Okay, smartass. I get it. But we're not here to talk about my extracurricular activities; we're here to talk about the girl."

"Exactly, the girl," Rose Double Dutched in. "I was with the girl that night at the restaurant—but you already knew that. This girl's name is Giselle Elizabeth Ignacio—but you already knew that too. The girl I was with is also your murder victim; they're the same person, lieutenant. . . and it doesn't seem like you knew *that*."

"Okay, this whole thing just got a whole lot more fucked up. They're one and the same? So are you're admitting that you were with her—the girl that just got killed, you're admitting that you slept with her? You are finished!"

"No! Hell no!" Rose rebutted, indignantly. "Don't you remember what I told you in the bathroom that night? I was getting information from her for my career. She was helping me with the Ash Wednesday murders case. She was my confidential informant."

"You can't have a *C.I.* You're a goddamn rookie and you violated department policy. Plus, I remember it now, you guys were all over each other in the courtyard. You had a sexual relationship with an underage girl. I'm going to collar you."

"You can't collar me! I didn't do anything wrong. I'm a cop!"

"You *were* a cop, use the correct tense," the lieutenant kneaded, agitating a sleep-deprived Rose.

"I didn't have a sexual relationship! Listen to me: It wasn't even like that. It was for my career; I was trying to close that case out. I can help you though. I can help you with one of your other cases," Rose pleaded, panting slightly. "I'm talking about the cop assault one. The one you came to my precinct and asked us about," he continued desperately.

Don't worry about that case. I'm gonna find out who those dirt bag cops are and they'll be turning in their badges too."

"What if I told you that I was in the car when the incident happened?" Rose lobbied. "That we drove past Rory's Alehouse and saw two *bosses* beating down some poor Asian man over a sewer grate?"

"What the fuck do you mean bosses?"

"Yeah, you're looking for cops right? The perps were *supervisors*. One of them was an executive."

"Oh, now I know you'll say anything to save your ass, you little rookie prick."

"I was there, check my memo book entries. I had a foot post and two old-timers picked me up and we patrolled around for a while. Then we saw this Chinese guy face down on the ground and this lieutenant and captain were just stomping on him."

"An *NYPD* captain and lieutenant?"

"Yes! An NYPD captain and lieutenant. I hate to snitch and all that crap but the poor guy was defenseless!"

"How come you didn't come forward sooner?" the lieutenant inquired. "And don't think you're off the hook because of that, we still need to know about you and the juvenile. I heard you cried like a baby when she died. Tell the truth, it's going to come out anyway: did you *tap* that young ass?"

"That's despicable!" Rose replied, wincing his face at the thought. "I didn't tap anything. I was crying because some asshole stepped on my goddamn hand, my hand is broken now," Rose informed, displaying his wrapped hand for his interrogator to see. "I don't know how she even got my number. But I was just writing a parking ticket when the call—"

"A parking ticket?" interjected the lieutenant. "You're talking about a parking ticket during a murder investigation? Is something wrong with your head?" the lieutenant posed, yelling now. "Are you out of your goddamn mind?"

"Check the time on the ticket!" Rose yelled over him. "It matches up. That's the exact moment that she called me. They were dealing guns and she wanted me to come in and make the arrest. Check the times, sir!"

Rose threw a rumpled copy of the parking ticket on the table. His monthly activity sheet was folded in four, inside the officer's copy, and landed on the table as well. Lieutenant Angulo carefully inspected both items.

"Let me see the call log on your phone, and what's this crap? Did you really have six arrests in March?"

"Seven," Rose corrected. "I forgot to add one on there. A bullshit weed collar."

"So I guess this is supposed to make you some type of hard charger, huh? What are you doing for an encore in April?"

"According to you I'll be somebody's bitch. I guess April really is the cruelest month."

"Who said that?" Angulo asked earnestly.

"Thomas Stearns Eliot. *T.S.*"

"Tough shit. Because by coming forward and identifying these members of the service you're probably putting two of your superiors behind bars."

"Well, that's the poison I'm picking. I'm no criminal. Maybe they shouldn't have been kicking the crap out of someone in the middle of the night."

"And the guys that drove you?" Angulo asked rhetorically, "they can kiss their pensions goodbye."

"Those guys are decent officers. I don't want to hurt them," Rose protested.

"Too bad. Everybody goes down. And your testimony makes you a rat."

"I'm no freaking rat. But letting those guys leave after the beating they gave that guy wasn't cool either. We're supposed to be better than that. *I* am better than that. But you said I had one chance to save my pathetic career, right? So I'm taking it."

"Yeah, self-preservation," Angulo mocked.

"I didn't sign up for this. Protect and serve? My ass. You had thirty witnesses outside that bar and you need me to snitch in order for you to solve your case. Yeah, you're really good at what you do."

"I'm just doing the same thing you did, no? You needed a snitch to solve your case too," Angulo manipulated with a smug look. "You had an informant, yeah? So now you're *my* informant. That's called irony. And this is called 'cloak and dagger'."

"Well, much more dagger than cloak I see."

"You're the one stabbing your boys in the back," Angulo potshotted.

"Well, the alternative is slitting my own goddamn throat, so excuse me if I *do* aim for center mass," fired back Rose, coming out of his chair and halfway across the table.

Rose would proceed to comb through a photo book with the lieutenant watchfully standing guard over him. He identified the culprits from that night's beating from their official department ID card photos, organized in a tidy binder like baseball cards. No one ever thinks when they're posing for that photo that it could lead to them winding up on the wrong end of a set of handcuffs. Rose avoided that end for the time being. He negotiated a deal to salvage his career and was now free to return home and try to reassemble his life from the pieces of fractured glass, memory, and morals that remained woefully intact.

When Rose arrived home early that morning, and darkness still had its grip on the sky, he reached for a small wooden cigar box, with one of the screws on the lid loose and producing a rattling sound. Once open, it revealed an encased NYPD detective's shield. An inscription beneath it read: "Detective First Grade Reinaldo Rose." Rose unfolded a yellowed newspaper article that read: "Hero Detective Slain in Bronx Gun Battle." Overcome with emotion, he quickly folded up the article and pulled out a note that he had written to himself on his lonely ride home on the number one train after the Tavern on the Green escapade.

> You have affected my heartbeat tonight and that must count for something. You have impacted my bones and set fire to my core. I am—under no condition—supposed to love you. But tonight I was not at all capable of doing what I was "supposed" to do. You have beguiled me with nothing more than transparent eyes and a heart that jumps out of your mouth when you smile. I have been disarmed and it appears to me that I am now yours to a degree, despite my ineligibility. I do not know how I lost every single advantage that I held over the situation, but I'm curious as to how curious you are to explore the power you now possess over me.

Rose read his own calligraphic handwriting and felt both ill and nostalgic in the same conflicted pulse. He grabbed a half-consumed bottle of pinot noir by the neck and swigged directly from the finish, mostly spilling it onto himself. He launched the bottle across the room, shattering it against a framed picture of the Brooklyn Bridge and the New York City skyline, enhanced by an orangey affect. Red drops rained, and glass crystallized—snowlike—and they were both blown back into Rose's face by a rogue wind that had broken into his broken abode. A huge incandescent question mark began to rise from the wooden planks of the floor. Rose reached for another half-finished bottle, and this time guzzled it completely. Flames danced in his living room like participants at a luau. Embers scattered into the air and then a chill settled into the shrinking living quarters. Rose explored his surroundings, disoriented, trying to separate the physical from the abstract. He shivered as beads of sweat baked on his forehead, and his temperature heated and he reddened with the blood cooking underneath his flush flesh. Rose pulled his gun out from its holster and raised it to the caving ceiling. He racked the slide and a round ejected. It suspended in the air, defying gravity in its unwillingness to spiral toward the ground. It just hung up there. Rose ejected his magazine and it slid out of the handle, parallel with his body until it hit his shoe. He kicked the clip into some distant region of his domain. With a single round left in the chamber, Rose raised his service weapon near his dizzying head. He lowered the barrel, but brought it right back to his temple. He reversed the position of the gun and stared down the barrel, where a hollow point 9mm round slept comfortably in the chamber, waiting to be awoken. The indented gold tip of the bullet was barely visible, but one could still make it out for what it was. It was death's messenger. Rose put the barrel into his mouth, lowered his lips onto the cold metal of his gun, and then . . . *BANG*!

Rose collapsed backward onto disarranged sheets, regurgitating wine onto his own face. His weapon bounced off the foam top of his sunken mattress and clanged onto the floor. His mind traveled and he dreamt, surrealistically. He envisioned that they were at an oasis atop a destitute wasteland. Christ himself, beardless and with an ash cross on his forehead, had descended down from heaven and onto a project rooftop to convert the urine soaked into roof gravel into champagne. This kicked off a Gatsby-themed party, attended by a few wraiths of smoke who swayed like clotheslines before full length mirrors, at the pulsating apex in the center of the slum. Giselle materialized, wearing feathers and pearls, and she set up two discarded public school desks and a folding table from the discount store as their dinner setting. The scene was backlit by a thousand multi-colored Christmas lights, including one particularly brilliant strand in the shape of a heart, blinking in pattern. Chicken wings and French fries were on the menu, written in graffiti on a red brick wall—in the dream Giselle discordantly referred to them as "caviar and blini." It was an opulent night sandwiched in between a fatal shooting and a staircase rape, neither of which Rose responded to—although he heard the transmissions—as he was fully invested in his last supper with Giselle. Song surrounded them and they clinked champagne flutes and toasted to trouble, dancing on the table until its legs caved in. Rose wanted to kiss Giselle, but didn't this time. After dinner, men dressed in ghost white forensic-collecting attire rappelled down from the water tank and kidnapped Giselle. She was then shoved into a human meat locker and the door was slammed shut by the medical examiner. In permanent black marker, the coroner wrote, "Giselle Elizabeth Ignacio," permanently. And she was no more. Rose was incapacitated at this point. And he could only watch in horror since he had been deprived of the use of his limbs by his mind's lurid straight jacket of a subconscious.

Rose awoke from this dream-turned-nightmare by the vibrating sound of his cell phone. The phone slid off the bed and Rose dove after it, folding up on the ground like an invertebrate. As he returned slowly to reality, he realized that the call was from Cecelia, not Giselle. He painfully hit "ignore" and then felt around his nightstand for the King James Bible, which reliably rested there. He tugged the Bible down to the floor by its built-in fabric bookmark and clutched it.

"Lord, I know in my heart that I am at fault for Giselle's death," Rose prayed, through tears, "and I will live with that forever. If there is a way for me to salvage this, please light the way. Forgive me, father, for the vengeance that I must seek and please protect me always."

Rose lied on his back and the tears rolled down the side of his head, pooling in his ear canal. He pressed the Bible tightly against his chest, holding on to his faith while pedaling with his legs toward the ceiling. He rocked a bit, from side to side, trying to shake out the pain that paralyzed him at this very moment. He looked skyward and inward, simultaneously, hoping that the hand of God could pluck him from the dire and damp depths of despair in which he backstroked feebly. Neither God nor grief could grant Rose any relief, and he experienced virtual death in that moment.

"The Lord . . . the Lord is my salvation. I will trust in him," he uttered into the leather cover, his trust fraying at the strands like a raggedy rope.

In civilian attire, Rose and Cheddar convened in an alley with a flickering street lamp feebly illuminating the two. A strained Rose sported a completely shaved head which, along with new scratches on his face, made him look almost completely unrecognizable.

"I can't believe you paid for that haircut," Cheddar belittled. "I have an electric razor that—"

"You know what we have to do now, right?" Rose interrupted.

"We don't have to do anything except sign out at the end of our tour. Do you remember that? Sergeant McMahon from the police academy," Cheddar reminded sternly.

"You know what I'm talking about," Rose muttered gravely, his top and bottom teeth never separating.

"What? Arrest the guys that killed her? We don't even know for sure who—"

"No!" Rose roared violently. "I'm done arresting people. We have to do to them what they did to her."

"Are you fucking *crazy*?" Cheddar asked, elongating the word "crazy" to its absolute limit. "You're out of control right now. Okay . . . I'm going to be honest: you look gone to me. *Gone*. Go on sick leave or use up your vacation time, but you can't be here anymore. How the hell did I.A.B. not modify you? You're a train wreck! Go home, *Brandon*. Or go see your girl in California. Let the detectives do their jobs now."

"The *detectives*? Is that a joke? I could fart in this alley and they couldn't figure out which one of us did it if we let them sniff our asses." Rose's face rumpled up and he yearned for something to throw. "Fuck them and fuck the gold shield!"

"Oh, now fuck the gold shield," Cheddar retorted. "You don't want the promotion anymore? Why? Because you took a bath in shit? Because your save-the-world mentality almost got you jammed up? You had your head so far up a teenage girl's ass, chasing the gold shield, that you forgot what we're actually here for. We're here to preserve life, right? Start by preserving your own."

"I know what we're here for," Rose fired back. "But I just need to get the guys that killed Giselle. They need to be dispatched to hell so the Devil can deal with them, like Garret said."

"Fuck Garret! He only cares about you making arrests so he can look better. What is he, some type of father figure to you or something?"

"Fuck you, motherfucker!" Rose erupted, with his fist cocked and poised to alter the arrangement of Cheddar's veiny, engorged face.

"Listen to me. If you go after these guys, if you *kill* these guys what do you think is going to happen to you? We talk about pissing on rooftops, but you're taking a shit on this badge, on this patch—on this entire uniform if you turn into one of the very same monsters that you hate. They're monsters and you aren't, okay? You're a good guy but you're throwing it all away now," Cheddar asserted passionately, prosecuting his own case now.

Rose teared up again. He struggled to find the words and inched closer and closer to the end of his shortening, tattered strand of twine.

"I'm not trying to disgrace this uniform. I love this shit. I love being a cop," Rose professed at a cadence that was alien to their debates. "But I just have to—"

"Become a vigilante? Become a *perp*? Listen to me please," Cheddar implored. "I'm your partner. If your dad was alive, he wouldn't approve of this. He might even bring you in himself. This isn't for you. You're an English teacher, you're a newspaper editor, you aren't a cop. If you wrote about this ordeal, you'd probably win a Nobel Prize or Pulitzer prize or whatever the hell it's called. You got caught up, I know, but she was just a street rat."

"She was my informant," Rose replied, a bit of craziness invading his eyes now.

"Exactly," Cheddar said, his tone softening. "Confidential informant. *Secret* informant. She doesn't look so secretive anymore. Fifteen-year-old girls squeal. It's what they do."

"She's sixteen," Rose corrected. "About to turn seventeen."

"She's zero because she's dead," Cheddar remarked crudely. "Tomorrow you'll be dead if you don't stop right here. Do you want to join the long list of fallen cops? People are coming for us anyway; you don't need to make their job easier."

Rose stared blankly at Cheddar but did not speak. Cheddar shook his head in disgust and then hugged his partner tightly. He squeezed him devotedly as Rose remained there, standing upright, not returning the embrace.

"Don't do it," Cheddar warned, his voice suddenly trailing off. "You're too good for this fucked up place. I don't want to say I knew a great guy. I want to say I know a great guy. Let me say I know somebody good and virtuous in this hell hole."

And with that he walked away, exposing an emotional side that was previously dormant. Rose didn't walk away. The boots he wore might as well have been made of rocks from the most muscular mountain. There was no budging him or his indefatigable boulder-like will that would only die if he did.

Rose retired to his Kingsbridge apartment, still stirring inside, feeling anything but restful. He paced apprehensively before reaching out to Cecelia.

"Cecelia, I'm having a breakdown. I've been hallucinating. I-I-I saw flames. I'm seeing shit again."

"Flames?" Cecelia questioned. "What are you talking about? In plain language. Why are you seeing flames?"

"Ce, I have blood on my hands. There's blood all over me. It's my fault!"

"Brandon, you're not making sense. Have you been drinking again? Why are you talking about blood on your hands? Answer me! Baby, what is going on?"

Cecelia yelled into her phone as pain etched new lines all over Rose's aging face. That face creased up as she called out her fiancé's name, but he was deaf to her cries and did not possess the vitality required to conjugate a response.

The following afternoon a severely compromised version of Rose hobbled into the detective squad offices at the fifty-first precinct. Rose gravitated toward the window where a bucket filled with water rested placidly on the sill. He dumped the bucket out, making sure he didn't accidentally soak any passersby or police officers in the process. Rose snooped around, taking in wanted posters and numbly feeling for dust on the over-stacked piles of detective case files with his fingertips. An old-fashioned .38 revolver and obsessed-after gold shield rested on a desk. Rose picked up the shield, still so in awe of it. He spun it as it reflected the light that was sneaking in through the half-opened windows.

"May I fucking help you?" Detective Jones asked rudely.

"I'm sorry," replied a startled Rose. "I just had a question for you guys." The detective didn't reply but Rose continued anyway. "I've been working on a case and I was wondering—"

"You're one of the news guys, no?" the detective jumped in. "How the hell are you working on a *case* if you're just a rookie cop?"

A look of defeat set in on Rose's face. He was in the position of a wounded boxer going into the twelfth round way behind on the scorecards. He didn't have much punch left or perhaps he was saving it for one last flurry.

"I'm sorry, pal," the detective offered, his chowder-thick Bronx accent pouring through as if out of a can. "That was wrong of me. I usually don't even talk to rookies but go ahead, entertain me."

"How can I get into an apartment if I have probable cause to believe that there are guns and murderers inside of it?"

"Wow," remarked the detective, astonished and interested. "That's pretty heavy stuff. You're gonna need a search warrant and the Emergency Services Unit it sounds like."

"There's no time for a search warrant, is there another way?" Rose probed.

"There's an old movie, a classic, right? In the movie the detective kicks the door in and pays a crackhead to say she informed them that the killer resided there. You ever seen that movie?"

"A movie?" Rose asked, rather dismayed. "Are you serious?"

"I'll give you one other way and then you can go back to your foot post and leave me the hell alone: *knock on the door*."

"Sure. And then what, they invite me in for tea and biscuits and say, 'By the way here is our gun arsenal?'"

"Listen, *assclown*, experience is a great teacher. You'd be surprised. Ring a doorbell once in a while, rather than holding up the street corner. If they open the door and something is in plain view: drugs, a *gun*, it's all fair game. *"Good ta' go*," as they say. You can always articulate the rest. There are many ways around the fourth amendment. You just gotta be creative. What are you, a goddamn millennial or something?"

The detective chomped on a dampening, torpedo-shaped cigar and blew bluish smoke into Rose's blue face, insultingly. Rose fanned away the exhaled smog.

"Thanks a lot, dick. Oh, and by the way: I dumped out your water bucket. Just because you're an old moth-eaten son of a bitch, who happens to be established, doesn't mean you should piss on those strivers who are young and ambitious. You were me one day. Around twenty years ago you were me."

Detective Jones pointed Rose toward the door, with his middle finger. When it shut behind him, Rose turned the first "t" in the word "detective" into an "f" with his pen. His act of vandalism only made him feel worse about himself and his sinking standards of behavior.

In uniform now, Rose reconvened with Cheddar on their impoverished post along Prospect Avenue. The prospects were high that Rose would do something desperate that night and the fraternal duo ping-ponged vis-à-vis this very troublesome matter.

"I just have to do one more thing and then, I promise, it's done," Rose insisted adamantly.

"You poor son of a gun. Can you just leave it alone and not tempt fate?"

"Fuck fate. Tonight is my last night patrolling in this cesspool. I'm out of here. I'm doing this for her."

"There you go again with that," Cheddar quarreled. "If you think heaven opened up and the angels cried when she died, you're smoking something. She probably went to the same hell all of us are going to. Heaven or hell, they can both wait. I wouldn't be in any rush to get into either one if I were you."

Lieutenant Garret interrupted the debate, cruising up slowly in his trademark unmarked sedan.

"All this talk of heaven and hell and I don't hear anything about collars," he pressured.

The two snapped to attention and saluted the impact lieutenant. They pulled out their memo books for his inspection and signature.

"I'm not here to scratch you, guys. I need a driver for tonight."

"Rose will drive you, *Lieu*. He's burnt out. Straight toast. He needs a break."

"Is that true, buddy?" the lieutenant corroborated. "I know you've been through hell recently."

"No, I'm good, *LT*," Rose denied. "I'm trying to collar up again tonight. Take one of these predators off the street."

"Atta' boy," encouraged Garret. "My worker's back. I'm thinking cop of the month for you in April maybe."

Cheddar attempted to push Rose into Garret's vehicle. Rose shoved Cheddar off of him and placed him in a headlock, spinning around until Cheddar stumbled to the ground.

"What the hell are you two doing?" scolded Garret. "You two are supposed to be fighting the perps, not each other. Jump in Cheddar, let's go."

The lieutenant pulled Cheddar into his car by his epaulet. Cheddar pleaded with Rose, mouthing "don't do it" through gritted teeth and the thick glaze over Rose's eyes. Rose removed his eight-point hat and Frisbee-d it into the back seat through the rolled down window. The lieutenant and Cheddar motored off into the corroding night. And Rose was, once again, alone under dim street lamps; their curved vertebrae bending even lower, struggling to illuminate him, with the dimming light of life pushing him into the closing corners of darkness.

Rose soldiered on into the black night, and when he arrived at the rooftop of 1805 Harmony Avenue, he shined his flashlight into the infamous elevator shaft. It appeared as if his body had been taken over by some other being as he stoically changed into blue jeans, a New York Yankees home jersey with the number two on the back, and a black knit ski cap. All of these items had been placed there ahead of the moment and were neatly folded and arranged in the hiding place of choice. He removed unnecessary items from his gun belt, leaving only his firearm, two extra magazine clips, a pepper spray canister and his department radio. Rose examined his handcuffs, sitting in their case, and flung them into the darkest section of the elevator room, making it clear that the campaign he would wage tonight would be of the scorched earth variety. He exited dressed completely in civilian attire, looking nothing like a cop, but everything like a man possessed and missioned to serve a frigid dish of revenge upon his foes.

Rose strode forward, marching boldly into what he believed would be beautiful violence. He knew inside him that bullets would adorn the air like fireflies in the summertime; their lead conspiring to light him up and return him to dust, like the bulbs of those beetles light up the dusk. Rose wasn't at war with the community but he was at war with specific members of the community who broke the law. If it came down to it he would give those adversaries luminescent organs as well. He had the firepower and he most certainly had the motive. Rose looked up at 711 Fairplace and measured himself against the building, which now appeared gargantuan and evil insofar as an edifice can. There he stood, on the precipice of battle, trying to get his mind to commit to what his body had to do. Everything else in life acts as a metaphor for what this would actually be, which is combat. He stepped into his decision and into the moment boldly, his heart having surprisingly outlived his mind which had all but perished when Giselle did.

CHAPTER X

Inside the dwelling of Rose's purpose, which burgeoned and dwindled conjointly, a new, older female had replaced Giselle as the employed lookout for the two underbosses. The braless twenty-something-year-old boiled potatoes on a stove, its flames scorching, heating the apartment more than the paint-shedding radiator actually did. An irritated, sinewy, brown and white pit bull barked ravenously, prepared to devour, and was chained to a well-worn steam pipe. His violent yap, along with the emanating hip-hop chants that rode a throbbing, synthesized beat created a sort of built-in bedlam within the apartment. Rose rang the doorbell and inexpertly impersonated a junkie. He bobbed and swayed, perhaps not realizing that he was loosening up his tense body to bob and sway away from the projectiles that he would have to elude to survive the untender night.

"Hey, pretty mama," Rose muttered, "Lemme' get some a 'dat smack. That good *manteca*."

The woman stared at Rose, the way he was attired, his overall appearance. He did not explicitly make a convincing customer and she would certainly know it if she saw one. She immediately noticed the pronounced bulge of Rose's service weapon at his hip as well as the silver chain attached to his shield around his neck and those intense eyes, which were focused and contained clarity, unlike your typical addict. The watcher attempted to slam the door on Rose's face, but he blocked with his foot, displaying his police pedigree, namely tactics 101. Rose forced his way in as she retreated into the kitchen yelling "five-o," warning the two drug dealers inside that a cop had invaded their hideout. Rose took one brave stride in, quickly scanned his environment, and charged forward with resolution at his back. The wooden floor boards buckled beneath him as the guardian beast leapt up and sunk his teeth into the meaty portion of Rose's forearm. A loud *clap* further alerted the occupants of the drug den as

Rose blasted a round into the eye socket of the four-legged monster. With the mix-breed's eye dripping out of its orbital like yolk from an egg, Rose kicked the crumpling canine in his muscular ribcage, breaking his toe and fatally stymieing its attack.

Reemerging now, the watch girl hurled the pot of boiled water onto Rose, prompting a death yell at deafening decibels. Water sizzled as Rose's flesh cooked in browning potato water. He instantly retaliated, emptying his pepper spray on her face, and then he muscled off a right hook that lifted and deposited the stand-in—feet exposed—into the next room, as if a house had just fallen on her. The first stage of the gauntlet complete, Rose paused for one second before resonant shots perforated the wall behind him. Fear now blanketed Rose as sheet rock dust sifted from the extemporaneous clouds that occluded the way out.

Rose dove for cover but took two angled shots to the chest, which were mostly absorbed by the front panel of his vest. He recalibrated, taking a moment to convince himself that this was the real thing and that he was in an actual gun battle. He rumbled forward like a locomotive, blowing smoke and abhorrence out of its smoke stack. Rose decisively returned fire against the bullets, which sailed past him like pellets of deadly leaden hail. He blasted off a piece of Greer's non-shooting hand and as Greer examined his missing appendages, Rose put a large cavity in the center of his chest. Rose was aghast at his work, biting his lip in angry trepidation before Puff *banged* away with his pistol, causing bullets to ricochet crazily and illuminate the apartment like a lightening bug colony had just been released into the air. Bullets fragmented the way the night had fragmented—in a way that could never be reassembled. Puff peeked out from around the corner, and Rose misfired with a few frenetic shots. Rose sprinted toward him, abandoning sound tactics, squeezing the trigger in asymmetrical tempo, and this time the rounds exploded into Puff's abdomen, lifting the gang member off the ground and folding him—chair-like—at the center. Airborne, Puff's buttocks crashed against the window behind him, shattering glass which sensationally rained down onto him like welder's sparks. Puff leaked blood from his lower back, neck, and gutted abdomen; Rose took a brief second to notice that he too was now bleeding. Rose panicked at the sight of his leaking life fluid.

"Officer shot! *Ten-thirteen* at 711 Fairplace!"

Puff squirreled out through the window and Rose leapt onto the ledge, glass gashing into his forehead, doing nothing to impede his red-hot pursuit. Hooves stomped corroded steps as the two stampeded up the potted plant-covered fire escape, disturbing drying laundry and reposed residents. Shots were exchanged at odd angles as bullets *zinged,* igniting sparks all over the over-painted fire escape steps. Both men's guns simultaneously emptied, ineffectually *clicking* as panic filled the brief recess. A race to reload commenced, and Rose hit the magazine release button on his weapon, using the combat reload technique he learned at the police academy. Puff failed to reload quickly enough, and he banged on Diablo's window distressfully as Rose filled the short distance between them. Rose tackled Puff through the window and the two entered Diablo's lair riding a stream of shattered glass, fracturing a few of their bones in the process. Rose squeezed his radio with all the strength he had left.

"I need a fucking *ten-thirteen*, Central! Top floor! Where the fuck is everybody?" he demanded, his shrill cry scraping against the turning stomachs of his summoned brothers.

As alarm swept through the precinct, Sergeant Valdez launched car keys in rapid-fire succession at officers surrounding the precinct desk. The cops snatched the keys out of the air like relay race batons and sprinted through the lobby. They bolted through the precinct's double doors, cracking the glass and causing the entrance to resemble a cracked dam. Blue gushed out, and they dashed out toward their vehicles poised to invade the damned domain where Rose was down, trying desperately not to die. As they departed, the American flag waved commandingly above them, thwacking in the breeze as if a declaration of war.

In Diablo's apartment, Puff was wilting slowly next to Rose. He reached around for a gun and this alone was enough to make Rose feel threatened again, and so he impetuously expedited Puff's demise. Rose advanced to the next room where he came face to face with the faces of murder. The shadowy men, who had taken on an almost mythological status, greeted Rose with something less than a warm greeting. The biting cold steel spoke just as soon as they did.

"Just the motherfucker I need," Diablo casually declared before ripping off more shots against Rose's fading body and withering spirit.

The bullets bombarded Rose, with approximately five ripping into the exposed areas of his frame. Rose caved into himself, taking a hard seat on the ground. His shooting hand was now incapable of squeezing, and his gun slipped from his grasp. Rose's tissue was atrophying before him, and the simple act of contracting was now an arduous chore. Writhing in a raging pain, Rose walked backward on his hands, dragging his butt, dripping blood and forming a trail for the crime scene unit to later process. He pulled his gun toward him by angling the tips of his feet inward and creating a pair of clumsy tongs with his legs. This just as more bullets flew over him, chewing apart the wall behind him. Sheet rock dust again fogged the air, and Rose took cover behind a reverberating column in the apartment. Crimson dripped from the numerous holes in his body, but he was still somehow able to calibrate thought.

"Come on out, pig!" yelled Kilo. "You come in here without an invitation, and you get shy once we show you the *heaters*. What kind of pussy shit is that?"

Rose examined his torn body tissue, inserting his right index finger into one of his still hot apertures. He disturbed the bullet mass inside of it and bubbling blood spewed out. Rose cried, his tears cleansing away the blood on his cheeks. His crimson mask washed away and his distinct facial features were once again discernible. He gripped his weapon with his left hand, recited a short prayer, and went after the men responsible for Giselle's death with hell bent determination.

"Kilo! Diablo!" Rose yelled, practically from the veins protruding from the sides of his neck. Rose stormed toward them, firing shots, and dodging the incoming fusillade. Mercifully, Kilo's gun jammed and Rose squeezed three shots into his enemy's face with his left hand. Kilo's face exploded like a watermelon hit with an axe and Rose sidestepped his leaky remains, still pursuing the leader.

Outside the war venue, patrol cars emptied and cops stormed the deadly erection. The structure had started to resemble a controlled demolition as bullets continued to detonate like compact bombs.

Diablo peeked around the corner, exposing himself to Rose. It was his biggest mistake of the night. Rose, weak hand trembling, held the discharging firearm and squeezed it and the bullets pounded into Diablo's chest like diminutive cluster bombs. This determinately decimated his chances of seeing tomorrow's light of day. They were now almost equally wounded and the fight had almost completely poured out of them at this point. They rested, like two boxers refusing to exchange. This was the clinch. They held to the walls that separated them as they clung doggedly to their waning existences. They breathed erratically, bleeding and stalling, with strength seeping out of their bodies as black police boots trooped up sordid steps.

Rose wondered why he had come this far. Was it really all for Giselle? Deep inside, he believed that he had constructed a museum of sorts in his heart for her. He collected moments—the precious moments he shared with her—which were framed by an uncategorizable type of love, and he hung them there, perhaps unevenly. And then suddenly, the museum was prohibited from collecting more artifacts, and it was closed. *He* was closed. And now Rose sought to close this nightmarish chapter like the hellish warrior that he positively was—in memoriam Giselle.

"Come out and surrender, you son of a bitch, and I'll let you keep your pathetic life!" he ordered.

"Who the fuck do you think you are?" Diablo interrogated. "You're just another cop on the verge of dying. You're going to bleed to death in my apartment and for what?"

Cops banged on the door like they had a bull accompanying them. They kicked at the doorknob and smashed the doorknocker and peep hole with their batons.

"You killed a sixteen-year-old, you fucking animal! There's fifty cops outside that are gonna light your ass up in a minute. ESU is coming, *motherfucker*, your days are over! Just tell me it was you so I know. Just admit it. Let me hear you say you did it. Say you killed Giselle, you *fuck*! Say it!"

Rose was rabid; he expectorated saliva and blood and venom and his last few breaths as he yelled at his tormentor.

"Giselle? Is that what this shit is all about? That little rat bitch?"

The door buckled as the inner doorknob fell to the ground and the hollow metal of the door bent under the duress of angry boots.

"You killed her, didn't you?" a sobbing Rose asked, before spitting up more blood. "Didn't you, Diablo or Kilo or whoever the fuck you are?"

"Diablo, *maricon*. Kilo's dead. And yeah, I launched her off the roof like the little snitch bitch deserved. But do you really think I'm gonna let some piece of shit cop arrest me?"

Rose ejected his magazine and replaced it with a full one. He kissed his hand and made the sign of the cross. Diablo also made the motion. Rose stood up, coming out from behind cover, and barreled madly toward Diablo. The door detonated behind him as particles of wall and dust and the metal of the hinges thrusted forward and seemingly propelled him as if he had activated a landmine. Diablo sidestepped Rose, who went crashing into furniture, further fracturing himself and splintering into small, unrecognizable pieces.

"See you later you fucking *puercos*," Diablo signed off, excusing himself from the battle that had just raged. The storming officers cleared the apartment, room by room, almost shooting Rose who resembled meat at a slaughterhouse.

"My hands are up, don't shoot," he gently begged, almost as an addendum.

And the cops didn't shoot, if you can imagine that.

Diablo escaped through the window where he collided with Cheddar who was waiting for him, gun drawn, on the fire escape. The two men danced and then a deafening *bang* was heard. Cheddar dove for cover, almost coming off the fire escape. Lieutenant Garret held his weapon in position after having fired a poetic fatal bullet into Diablo's left breast. Diablo bent over onto the fire escape railing, and then the weight of his torso carried his lower body over the edge and into a terminal freefall. His body *clanged* as it collided against the bottom of an empty garbage dumpster, reverberating into the long-lasting memory of that savage day.

"May he rot in hell," declared Garret. "Son of a bitch perp."

Diablo perished in the dumpster, next to Giselle's backpack. Rose crawled on to the fire escape, his clothing shredded, and finished his life by curling into Cheddar's arms. Cheddar held his partner up to the crescent moon, its glow golden and casting a hazy luminosity which met Rose's eyes before they closed for the endmost time. He expired on the fire escape after escaping hellfire if only to achieve the most pyrrhic of victories. Garret completed the trinity by embracing both Rose and Cheddar as the three formed a tight, trying triangle. He held his young cops together as the officers in the apartment watched the embrace through the glassless window frame and their tears.

"*Lieu*, that's my partner," cried Cheddar. "That's my partner."

An NYPD helicopter chopped at the air now, flying over the location of Rose's demise.

"Aviation Central, can you advise if we are still needed," the pilot asked through noisy, buzzing blades that made his radio transmission moot, as if it wasn't already.

"One lieutenant, Central, have them go *ninety-eight*. The perps are apprehended."

"Okay, Lieutenant. What about the officer who called the eighty-five?" Central asked.

Garret pressed the button on the side of his radio, but words ceased to come out.

Rose was placed in the hands of the officers inside the apartment, who carried him down the stairs, each one making sure that they held a piece of the fallen officer's body in a ritualistic, zigzagged descent to the ground level.

In the dumpster, a young, enterprising officer pulled out a backpack and opened it. Inside of it, he found the guns that were used in the Ash Wednesday murders. A copy of *The Catcher in the Rye* was tucked in there as well, complete with a dedication on the inner front page:

"To my favorite policeman future detective Brandon Rose. Thank you for loving me. I know that you did ~ G.E.I."

A small red heart ended the memo.

As officers scavenged through the minefield that was Diablo's apartment, a cell phone rumbled next to a bullet shell casing. The officer handed the phone to Lieutenant Garret. The platoon commander answered to a low, pleasing voice.

"Baby?" she asked as sweet and tenderly as humanly possible.

"This is Lieutenant Garret," he said professionally. "I have something I need to tell you."

Cecelia's precious brown eyes shut closed as vitality departed her body. She tumbled to the ground, her cell phone twirling across her room in California like a ninja star. Her fall occurred as Rose arrived at St. Barnabas Hospital to be picked apart on a chilly operating table. The surgical staff converged on Rose, but it was all just a sad formality at this point.

A powerful bright light immersed Rose's body. It zoomed through a long, narrow, white tunnel. Something gold was seen: the coveted gold NYPD detective's shield. It glowed. The badge that Rose desired so badly—obsessed over—shone so nicely. The word "detective" looked so prestigious, and at the same time so immaterial. The nameplate underneath it read "B. Rose." It was Rose's last police dream, his *detective hopes* once again coming true before this narrator lost all insight into his consciousness and was relieved of his heartbreaking assignment. The light had gone out now and Rose was dreaming in darkness.

Rose would go on to sleep in a casket of understated elegance, paid for by the Patrolmen's Benevolent Association. His mother, Ana Rose, and his fiancée would meet under the golden statue of an angel at Pelham Bay Park on Easter Sunday. On that Resurrection Sunday, small children toted colorful Easter baskets and embellished multi-colored eggs. Birds chirped harmoniously, representing the new life that spring brings and scattering music in their flight. The grass was green and lush and lavish silvery clouds swam laps across the cerulean blue sky.

"He was pronounced at 12:01," Ana Rose pointed out. "He died on Good Friday."

"I don't even know how to process that," replied Cecelia.

The two women wept in each other's arms.

"He made detective," Rose's mother leaked, sadness sinking her down curving posture. She would never completely grasp what those three words meant to her son. "The commissioner appointed him to the rank today. After the investigation into his death is complete there's a possibility that they'll even name a street after him," his mother disclosed proudly and sadly. "They just need to look into his actions to see if he violated any department policies. But I know my son."

"I wish he never got that detective badge. He would still be here. And now I can't stop thinking about the memories we'll never make," Cecelia shared, herself visualizing memories they did create in that precise solemn reflection.

Mrs. Rose, still very much a mother—despite losing her only son—consoled an inconsolable Cecelia.

At the funeral, bagpipes played at near-deafening volume as an endless row of cops paid their respects to the newly minted detective's body. Six officers carried the coffin as Cheddar escorted Cecelia into the grand Catholic church. The stained glass adorned lancet windows and ornamental scalloping distinguished the Gothic Revival landmark from all the other houses of worship in Washington Heights as it proudly rose from the huddle of small walkups that surrounded it. Lieutenant Garret, looking regal in his dress uniform, led Mrs. Rose by the hand. Every officer in attendance wore a black mourning band over his or her shield. An electrifying helicopter fly-over closed the somber day as rain began to pour onto the sea of blue, standing by the thousands in perfect formation outside the church. The spontaneous downpour splashed up water against those classy dress blues and caps the way raindrops at a beach splash up water against insurgent waves. But the ocean of blue didn't budge; they all let the rain soak into their uniforms, darkening them in color, and providing some type of a cleansing sacrament that no one who isn't a cop could fully understand.

At Rose's apartment that night, Cecelia inspected her appearance in front of a slightly distorting mirror in her fiancé's bedroom. She brought Rose's blouse close to her nose and inhaled deeply. She could still smell the patchouli and white musk base notes of his cologne and that gave her a sliver of life. She slipped on his eight-point hat and adjusted the cap device, which bared Rose's shield number on it. She outlined the numbers "1004" with her slim, feminine fingers, tracing over them repeatedly. Cecelia gripped a fragrance bottle, stepped back and wound up like a pitcher. The bottle shattered the mirror as fragments rained down leaving only the wooden frame intact, shaking angrily. Cecelia cried there, alone, recalling the question mark formed by candles on the evening that he proposed to her. She wondered what life would have been like if she hadn't gone to the other side of the country to study. She clung tightly to Rose's cap and to the slowly evanescing image of him on his best day and her favorite day. She had questions that would forever remain unanswered, and she reached for

Rose, still present in that apartment, in the spiritual realm. Rose embraced Cecelia in the apartment, the temperature warming as if the engagement candles had been lit anew, and then a breeze traveled through, disturbing things that weren't weighed down. He was there somehow; somehow Rose was present with her.

I will always remember Brandon Rose—subject one—fondly, in spite of his apparent thorns. Rose was someone who is something you simply don't see every day. He was operatic, yet calm. Polished, yet jagged. Rose was a boutonniere with spikes, pinned to a Montblanc tuxedo by a rusty drywall nail. He unpremeditatedly ignited a small fire in Giselle's heart, and didn't possess the means to extinguish the inferno to which it grew. He opened up a young girl's envelope in a way that no one ever had before, and made her feel valued for the first time. This awoke her and him. Yes, Rose strayed from Cecelia fleetingly and certainly longer emotionally, but he loved her; I know this at my core. He kissed these two vastly different souls beneath the same luminescent moon, under completely different, nebulous circumstances. *Circumstances*, they make all the difference when trying to judge a man as a good one or an inadequate one. Rose earned a true-blue friend in Cheddar, fancied a father figure for himself in Lieutenant Garret, and made himself the unlikeliest companion imaginable in the loveable minx, Giselle. He gave birth to a bold dream for her, and gave her hope, out of his own dream of becoming an NYPD detective. It was complicated, if only because the delicious complexities that often accompany taboo love usually are.

Rose sacrificed his career, in essence scorching the path back, and put Giselle on his arm on that life-changing nocturne at *Tavern*. He wore her on his wrist like the most charming, sparkling charm. And that was the very highlight of her life, before her ghastly death. He lived with that pain until he died with it. I learned that Rose had gone through life collecting such charms on an imaginary bracelet. They were people, memories, losses—like his dad—all amassed like diminutive amulets that he wore beneath his rolled-up sleeve. Some of these were scuffed, some dented, some missing the jewel like the tiny stone that delineates the elephant's eye, but still there, dangling off the bracelet. Rose kept them all, discarding none, a constant reminder that shiny, sparkly, beautiful things have a way of becoming tired old relics drooping off your wrist, missing an eye. But still you wear them. And Rose wore that glimmering gold badge—the one he bled for, gave his life for—inside that oak box in the un-mowed grass where he lay. It didn't matter in the end, but what in life does matter in the end? His life mattered to me enough for me to tell the story of his vivid, ambitious, overreaching *police dreams*, since his boat drifted off course and didn't make it home so he could tell it himself. We make mistakes; we certainly are not perfect. However, we are good and we blindly run into harm's way to protect all lives, sometimes even giving our own. That's the thing about being a police officer: you don't always come home. Sometimes you die when you wear this uniform. Like the fallen heroes in New York and Dallas and Baton Rouge. And no one marches for you when you die. Except your brothers and sisters in blue, who get into *formation* and march on, on your behalf.

So we march on, boots against the opposing political current, against crime and the bad guys; we borne the thin blue line, the line that never ceases, never recedes, and beats on like memory—and the heart of a Rose.

Made in the USA
Lexington, KY
10 July 2017